Day & Night in Limbo

Jean Tardif Lonkog

Langaa Research & Publishing CIG
Mankon, Bamenda

Publisher:
Langaa RPCIG
Langaa Research & Publishing Common Initiative Group
P.O. Box 902 Mankon
Bamenda
North West Region
Cameroon
Langaagrp@gmail.com
www.langaa-rpcig.net

Distributed in and outside N. America by African Books Collective
orders@africanbookscollective.com
www.africanbookcollective.com

ISBN: 9956-792-62-4

DISCLAIMER
All views expressed in this publication are those of the author and do
not necessarily reflect the views of Langaa RPCIG.

Chapter 1
Go or Stay?

On June 16, 2008, I arrived in Yaounde from China. The recruitment of teachers into the public service had been launched. I had three days to apply. My little sisters Marie-Claire and Angel put together my documents for the recruitment. I was not taking this seriously, because my intention was to pick up another entry visa and return to China, for I did not come to Cameroon to stay. My sisters however, aware of all my instability in China, did not want me to return. I have written of what I went through in China in my first book "The Black Man and His Visa."

My sisters compiled and successfully deposited my documents on June 18. The government extended the closing date for about a week, but my sisters did all so I was able to meet the first deadline. In the end, I was a candidate for the batch of teachers recruited in September 2008.It was obligatory to choose two Northern Regions and one Southern Region. Nevertheless, it was clear that most of the teachers would be posted to the North, because it is a priority zone for the government and the educators in the country. Education is still backward in the three Northern regions of Cameroon. These are North (Garoua), Far North (Maroua) and Adamawa (Ngaoundere). The government wants to send more and more teachers there to build up the region. However, teachers are reluctant to go up North for reasons such as the hot harsh climate, the lack of water and electricity in most of the rural areas, plus the distance from home. Like most of the other candidates, I chose North, Adamawa and West.

Despite my possible recruitment, I did not give up my attempt to obtain a visa and return to China. I had applied for admission into a Chinese Traditional Medicine College. They accepted my application and sent an invitation letter to me by email. I printed the letter and went to the Chinese Consulate in Douala. They rejected it saying I should ask the school to post to me a stamped invitation letter. I shared this information with the college, and they said in August they had posted me the letter. However, I waited impatiently for the letter until I never received it. I wrote to them and informed them I did not receive it. Even by the end of September, I had still not received it. They insisted they had posted it to me. It was only after one year, that is in October 2009, that the relative whose address I used brought me a letter saying, "This is your letter, usually things do not go missing, we only forget to hand them over." When I wanted to ask how he forgot to hand me such an important letter, he had turned and was already leaving. I only spotted his back five meters away from me.

I was in the village until September 2008, when my sisters told me from Yaounde that the result of the recruitment was already published. I asked them to look at the list and tell me if my name was on it. They told me I was to work in the North Region and in Government School Carrefour Poli. In a country of mass unemployment, this was an opportunity for work. There are teachers who have been living in the country for many years and have not had the opportunity for employment. I applied in the nick of time and had a job. More so, many who deposited their documents were not recruited. I was very confused. Should I go for this job or keep fighting to receive my invitation letter and return to China? What should I do? I could seize an opportunity in hand or keep waiting and perhaps end up losing all. I finally decided to go to the North and work there as a teacher. After all, my invitation letter had failed to reach me

Chapter 2

Arrival in Carrefour Poli

We travelled by train from Yaounde and arrived in Ngaoundere where the train route ends. The journey was difficult. The number of people in our wagon was twice the number of seats. People and luggage blocked the pathways. The toilets also were full of people and luggage. God alone knows what happens to people who want to answer nature's call. For these reasons, I am always careful not to drink much water or eat much food before boarding the train.

We left Yaounde at 6:20 pm and arrived in Ngaoundere the next day at 3 pm, spending thus more than twenty-one hours covering the distance of about 1000 kilometres. The train goes at an average speed of 50 kilometres per hour. If we compare that to the modern high-speed trains recently built in China, which go 350 km/hour, then the Cameroon train is the Chameleon, or else a tortoise. If it were the high-speed Chinese or European trains, traveling from Yaounde to Ngaoundere would take just about three hours. We all work hard and hope Cameroon becomes an emerging economy so our standards of living improve and we too enjoy the good life. If the modern Chinese and European jet trains were to come here, it would mean breaking down the whole rail network and rebuilding it. If any Cameroonian is thinking of this kind of high-level project, he should keep it to himself because the government is busy with other things.

We would have reached Ngaoundere a few hours earlier however if our train had not knocked down a cow. Contrary to tales of old people in the villages about the train not being able to stop no matter what, our train did stop. It seems as if some people in the train were prepared for the accident. They pulled out long knives and rushed from the train. In compliance with the Captain of the train, they slaughtered the cow and shared the meat among themselves. The owner of the cow vanished because he feared having to pay fines for allowing cattle to stray onto the railway.

Many things can happen to delay a train. My uncle told me that once when he was travelling, the wagon he was ingot disconnected from the locomotive. His wagon halted, and the passengers saw how the rest of the train was advancing. It took some hours before the repairs were complete and they could continue the journey. The same uncle told me how one day in his first class wagon, a man, maybe mad, or if not made certainly very wicked or possessed by demons, pulled out a slaughterhouse knife and slaughtered a sleeping man who might have lost his life. The slaughterer was bitten to death by the rest of the passengers in the train. It took much time to bring order to the chaos in the train.

From Ngaoundere, I took a bus toward Garoua. Carrefour Poli is located on the main road between Ngaoundere and Garoua, approximately 100 kilometres from Garoua and 180 from Ngaoundere. When I arrived in Carrefour Poli, I asked for the school and went there. I presented myself to the headmaster, Mr. Goyoko Celestine, a short man in his mid-fifties. He and the other teachers were happy to receive me. The school was a six class school but had only three classrooms, built with sticks and grass. A modern building comprising two classrooms was under construction.

The first thing I realized was that there was no electricity. For this reason, I decided I would go and live in Gouna, which is four kilometres from Carrefour Poli. Gouna is still a village but a little more developed than Carrefour Poli. I went there with the headmaster to look for a house where I would live. He first showed me a room in his home where, if I liked it, I could live temporarily. I looked at the small room, and it seemed as if part of it was collapsing and as if rain leaked inside it. I told him it was better we go around the village and see if we could find another room. As we went round, no buildings he showed me were better. All hopes for a room were dying down. I saw one that looked better and pointed it out, but he told me it was not for rent. It seemed he knew everything about the houses in Gouna. I pointed at the next one and said, "Look, sir, there is a nice house."

He replied with a deep voice in French, "That is the hospital." We kept going, and I pointed out another place. Here plied, "That is the Lamido's palace" (the chief). I wanted to call his attention to the next place, but I spotted an Islamic religious symbol (the moon with stars) on top of the building, which indicated it was unquestionably a Mosque. We continued and finally found an acceptable place. We negotiated the monthly rent at 10 000 francs ($20) for the two small rooms. Comparing the house quality in a village, it was expensive in Cameroonian standards but I had not much choice. I asked about electricity. The property owner said electricity was not his business and that I had to arrange with somebody that had a generator to supply me lights. When he replied like that, I understood there was no electric supply in Gouna either. Therefore, I told the headmaster that we had better return to Carrefour Poli. There was no need for me working and living four kilometres away, where I do not have electricity. I felt in limbo.

Arriving in Carrefour Poli, it was not very easy for me to find a room. I lived in the school President's home for the first month. I had to find my own room from the second month. They showed me a room attached to a bar. There were many rooms there. Travellers rent the rooms to stay the night or just to rest for a few hours. I rejected to live in that kind of a place because of all the noise and music.

When I refused this place, people told me of a certain room with a lot of excitement. "A room, roofed with zinc! The English Teacher will live there!" They were excited because almost everyone lives in thatched houses. The few rooms roofed with zinc are in the Carrefour or main intersection itself or near the road they use for businesses, especially bars. We finally reached the room, but I found nothing to be excited about. There were two rooms, and a young man was living in one of them. The people asked me to occupy the other one. First, with all the heat in the North, the room had no window. The door was made of zinc, and there was a big hole in it. There was no lock on the door either from the inside or outside. One wall of the room protruded outward forming a "C" like shape, as if it could collapse at any time. Some of the nails holding the zinc had fallen out so that the least wind caused a loud noise. I asked for the latrine, and they led me behind the house; there was the pit latrine. As we approached, a goat emerged from it. The goat had run away from the strong sun and was resting inside. Probably, the latrine was less than a meter deep with a wide mouth. The villagers gave me the assurance that the young man occupying the other room would fix up the toilet, and I had to be paying my rents of 2500 francs ($5) to the boy every month. Someone rumoured to me that a military man owned the house, and that he abandoned it to the young man's father and left.

I had agreed to live and work in Carrefour Poli. I had to live somewhere. Therefore I accepted to live in this house. I lived there for the whole of that academic year. However, in the North, in between the month of February and May, temperatures are very high and places are very hot. I would have left my door open as I slept in the night if I had a bed. But that whole year I spread my mattress on the floor. There are many snakes and leaving the door open while lying on the floor might be dangerous. It was not easy to live in a room without a window. In addition, there was a grinding mill in front of the house emitting toxic carbon monoxide. One day, this gas filled my room. This smoke awoke me at night during deep sleep and I was almost suffocating. The heat was so much and I could not breathe well. The next day, I went to Garoua, and from that night, I suffered from a cough that lasted two months.

The long holidays finally came, and I left. I returned in September in time for the school reopening. When I arrived, the young man living in the house told me I no longer had a place to live in the house. A colleague was going to help me look for a new place. We decided I should live with him temporarily. We went to get my luggage from the young man in my former house. He had to open the door for me to carry my luggage, but he was on the road loading vehicles. He and my colleague were speaking in the dialect, and I did not understand what they were saying. Suddenly, a quarrel broke between them and I saw my colleague launching blows like Mike Tyson on him and shouting. We finally went home and brought out my luggage. I slept in my colleague's home that night. There was a visitor's room where one of his visiting relatives was living. We slept on a large mat on the floor. The door had no cover. Although I slept with my trousers and socks on, mosquitoes found blood to suck that night.

Because of the mosquitoes, I had to abandon this room the next day to join another friend, Mr. Zamba, in his one-room house. He was a parent-employed teacher in the same school where I was teaching. Insecticide smelled everywhere in his room. He told me he always sprayed his room to scare away snakes. Every night before sleeping, I pointed my torch under the bed to observe. He asked why. I replied, "To see if there are any snakes, that might be planning to launch a surprise attack at night when we are asleep."

He laughed and said, "While you sleep on the bed, you are afraid of snakes, but I who sleep every night on the floor is not afraid of snakes." However, the truth was that, if not for the fear of snakes, I would have preferred lying on the mat on the floor. There were potholes all over the bed. It was layered into mountains, planes and valleys, all on a small bed. Sometimes, waking from a nightmare, I would realize that my head was inside a pothole and my legs hanging off the mountain. That must have reversed my body's energy flow thereby causing me those nightmares. Sometimes, I would wake up lying straight in a valley of undulating surface. I lived on this bed for a week and left.

My friend later got married to a girl of about sixteen and as I saw, he did not bring a new bed or another mattress into that house. Life is very hard; as a parent-employed teacher, he earned just 15 000 francs ($30) a month. Unfortunately, the young wife passed away after three years in marriage leaving behind no child. If certain levels of hardship persist and there is no end to it, human life will be short. How can a woman conceive on a very low kind of diet and a very poor bed of that nature? She finally suffered from enema where the entire body swelled. As they carried her to the hospital, probably for the first time in her life, it was already late and she passed away.

I next lived in a tiny two-room apartment with a zinc roof that resembled the back of a supernatural frog painted with silver. I stood and looked at the house and cried Jesus of Nazareth, lead me in! I am sure he did because I survived the snakes, scorpions, bats and centipedes there. The villagers were very satisfied with it, and the news continued to go round that the English teacher was to live in a roofed two-room apartment. There were so many holes and openings in the house. I personally made mud and blocked most of the holes at least from ground to a higher level up. There were two tiny windows, but the inner room was still dark despite the window. I decided to sleep in the parlour instead of the inner room because it was so dark there I could not see the snakes, centipedes and scorpions except with a lamp or torch.

The man who owned the house lived in the city, so I met his son to whom I had to pay 2000 francs ($4) a month. This money is small, but for those villagers, having money every month end helps a lot. Even I, a teacher, comparing what I earn to the price of food, medical care, transport from my hometown, participation in social activities, research and everything that I do to do my work successfully, the salary is very small. I work to be able to eat and not starve to death. If I were to start thinking of carrying out projects like building a house, buying a car and opening bottles of beers every day, I would catch hypertension. Those beautiful things are out of my reach, so why give myself sleepless nights yearning for them? Some rare people however have the opportunity to enjoy them but still let them go. When I watch how our new Pope Francis 1, at the age of 76, prepares his food by himself, is this not wonderful and a powerful example for humanity? He goes beyond material comfort.

When I first entered my two-room apartment, I spotted, hanging on the wall in the darkness of the inner room, a large framed photo of an important politician. The picture had stayed there for many years untouched. It needed serious cleaning. I went to it and tried to lift it off the wall. As soon as I touched the frame, I heard a terrible noise. Birds flew past me touching my ears and face with their wings. They were uncountable. I realized they were bats. You have to be careful in the North. Instead of flying creature, it could be snakes; a snake can hide even under a leaf or a small piece of paper.

One night as I held my lamp in my hands, I almost stepped on some very shinny darkish thing. It was about twelve centimetres long. I first thought it was a snake but soon realized it was a centipede. Its skin was so hard that I had to hit it several times with a piece of wood before it died. I hung it outside, and my neighbour saw it the next morning and said he had heard me hitting something last night. I killed uncountable numbers of scorpions in this room.

One day I returned from work very tired and not feeling very well. Maybe malaria would come or maybe abdominal discomfort. I decided to lie on my bed and let the body rest. I lay on my back, looking at the ceiling. My eyes fell on something in a crack, above the inner door. It was the skin of a snake. I alerted my neighbour, who came with others. I asked them what to do. They said, "Nothing, do nothing." I asked how is it there is nothing to do. They said if a snake peels its skin, it does not live in that same place again. To them, there was nothing to be excited about. I told them I wanted to leave the house. They laughed and asked if I should leave my room just because of a snakeskin. The crack where the snakeskin was opened right up to where the wall met the roof. I asked for help to break open the crack. When we found nothing, they reaffirmed what they had told me, that the snake was no longer in my room.

I thought later that these inconveniences about housing were not good and healthy for me. Therefore, I met the village chief and asked for a small piece of land to build my own house. The chief responded well and showed me a small piece of land near the school. I built my room on this piece of land. I made the room large enough with two big windows. I also made seven small openings of ten by twenty centimetres close to the roof for more ventilation and fresh air. With a large room with many openings, the intensity of heat greatly reduced. I thatched the roof with grass too because, thatched roofs are not as hot as zinc roofed houses. I was comfortable in my room. I was able to sleep and stay indoors at all times despite the heat. I sealed the small openings and windows with mosquito nets. I made sure there were no openings or holes anywhere, to prevent snakes from entering the house. For the fresh air, I let my windows stay open twenty-four hours a day, seven days a week. Though my room was still hot, it was not as hot as the other places I lived.

Despite the heat in the North, people do not build their houses with large and many windows. Most of the rooms do not have windows, and if at all they do, the windows are tiny. Where are the architects of the North? But do we need architects to tell us rooms need windows for fresh air and ventilation? This is still a mystery to me.

Although I loved my room, one night something happened, an unforgettable affair that toed me out of my hard-earned room. I never dared lived in it again. Until now, I fear to step inside the room even for a few seconds. We shall talk about this unfortunate, unforgettable and embarrassing incident in a later chapter.

Chapter 3
Life without Electricity

At night, insects gather around the brightest lights they find. The same could be said for the people of Carrefour Poli. There is no electricity in the village, but two of its inhabitants own generators, which they use to operate bars.

They do not run these generators every day. They run them on market days and on days like March 8 (women's day) and days of national festivities like February 11 (youth day), May20 (national day), and the list goes on. On these kinds of days, they have many customers who drink much beer, thus much money comes in. Three years ago, there was a serious fight amongst two women during the March 8celebrations. One woman claimed another woman was trying to slash her husband. They fought, and the "Hardo" (village chief) ended up judging and resolving the matter. He banned the extravagant celebrations of March 8 in his village. So much drinking and dancing was thus forbidden on subsequent March 8 days.

In the nights where the generators are not started, people go to their local markets where they gather in numbers between twenty to one hundred people under big trees and drink the locally brewed beer call "bily bily." Sometimes spontaneous and periodic fights do breakout in these marketplaces. Two enemies may fight; one runs home and returns with a cutlass, and the other rushes to his own home and returns with a knife or a sword. If there is no luck and they meet each, there might be a clash of the titans. Blood may flow. At this point, each of them aims at slashing life out of his enemy.

During the evenings where there is electricity or not, the BIRs (rapid intervention force soldiers) enjoy sitting in front of one of the bars. This bar's ground is a little elevated. All the buses from Ngaoundere to Garoua stop in front of the bar. All the passengers spot the BIRs wearing a singlet with shorts or a pair of jean trousers. They sit and face the road. Between their legs stands a bottle of beer. It is always there. Sometimes I thought being able to consume beer might be one of the criteria to be a BIR soldier. The BIR soldier, even if he is alone, seems to be smiling. Is it a sign that he is happy? Is it a sign he is satisfied with his job? Is it a sign of alcohol intoxication? Is it a sign to show how he had successfully prevented a fight somewhere? Only he knows, but one thing is clear. Among the unemployed poor villagers, he has to smile. Why smile? Because at least he is employed and better than all others around him are. The villagers envy the BIR soldiers. They are young and vigorous. They have taken all the women. In a couple years, the result shall be clear before the eyes of everyone. The seeds they are nursing should be getting ready to germinate, and many children carrying BIR blood will be running around. The BIR soldiers are not stable. The government moves them from place to place, and who knows what shall become of these still to be born children when their BIR fathers are not to be found.

When there are interesting football matches, especially when Cameroon is playing, we all gather in one of the bars and watch. We each pay 100 francs to watch a match, and there is always a lot of noise. There is no way to stop the crowd; you take the noise or you go and miss the match.

In those bars, funny things sometimes happen. In the good days when I used to take beer, I held a small bottle of Guinness in my hands and watched an interesting thing happen. There was a man sitting with his bottle of beer standing in front of him. A man and his wife came in dancing. They had no drinks. I watched the woman leave her husband and go to the man sitting. After greetings and a small chat, I saw the man handed his bottle to the woman. The woman danced around while drinking from it. When she met her husband in one corner, he seized the bottle and started emptying it. I saw the eyes of the owner of the bottle widen as he watched what was happening. He finally got up and rushed to the couple to rescue his bottle, but it was too late. He expressed serious anger and cursed the couple. Maybe this man could only afford this one bottle for that evening. The couple could not afford a beer, but they dare not stay away indoors on a night where there was light, for it might be a week or more before an opportunity like that one comes up again.

To charge the phone is a serious problem. A young man with a generator that cost about 40 000 francs ($80) uses it to charge phone batteries. He charges every phone for 150 francs. It is possible he makes quite a bit of money, as you may see about forty batteries or phones charging at one time. However, how long may this opportunity last? You may hear that the generator has broken down, or that the young man has moved to another village. Nothing is permanent.

It is not very easy for the inhabitants of Carrefour Poli to live without electricity in their homes. In southern Cameroon, in areas where there is no electricity, there are kerosene lamps in almost every household. However, here in the North, only a few households have lamps. As for others, when their flashlights go bad or when there are no batteries, they live in the darkness.

I once asked a friend why they do not have kerosene lamps. He said, "Since the lights came, we stopped buying lamps." I was surprised at this response. We all live in Carrefour Poli, and there are no lights, yet he comes with this statement beginning with "since the lights came." He laughed and said he meant these kinds of flashy lights and torches powered by batteries, some of which are almost as bright as electric bulbs. The people of Carrefour Poli are satisfied with darkness and hope for no lights very soon. I never heard any of them mention anything related to an electricity project for their village. Yet Carrefour Poli is in Lagdo subdivision where hydroelectricity is generated.

Chapter 4
Living without Water

Water is hard to find in Carrefour Poli. There are wells in the rainy season, but we all know that well water is not very good. Dumped inside these wells are old pieces of wood, clothes and all kinds of rubbish. The rainy season is very short, from June to September, and maybe one or two rains in October. The rains fall only occasionally in these four months of the rainy season. When the dry season begins in October, the wells start drying up almost immediately, and they dry up completely before January.

There is a small river down the valley to the east of Carrefour Poli. Everyone goes down into the valley to fetch a bit of water, but the river too dries up at the beginning of the dry season. However, because the riverbed is wet, the villagers dig small holes of about 70 centimetres wide all along the river's course. Water collects in the holes bit by bit and people use bowls to carry it, but this water is not healthy. Water has no colour, yes this one does. It is always whitish or darkish. For the inhabitants of Carrefour Poli, however, there is nothing wrong with the water. When I boil this water to drink it, people watch with amazement and think there is a mad man living amongst them. My colleagues, teachers native to Carrefour Poli, teach methods at school of purifying water but they never boil their water. They never treat or purify their water the way they teach to the children, This is no surprise. Everywhere you see people teach what it is not their experience or what they do not practice. Ministers preach goodness and patriotism but end up in prison for embezzlement? Priest preach goodness, fidelity and all kinds of virtues, but look what is happening in churches around the world. The new Pope Francis 1 has an uphill task to reconcile sexual abuse by priests and the morality of the church. What is important is that everyone follow his or her own conscience. Everything is in limbo. We are in limbo.

In March, no matter the amount of digging, no water comes out of the riverbed. The villagers have to seek this precious liquid elsewhere. The village of Bella is not very far from Carrefour Poli, about five kilometres away. Young men with vigour go with trucks and carry water from there and sell it. Each truck can take about eight twenty-litre containers. The young men sell each drum for150 francs. Therefore, each trip can earn them 1200 francs ($2.50), and a strong person can make four trips a day. Some men use their bicycles to get water from Bella. I once visited the water source there. It is a small spring. It supplies the whole village of Bella and Carrefour Poli during the months of March, April, and May. It is a spring, but because so many people got here every day, the water is no longer clean. The water has to collect in a pool for people to carry it. People fight to get to the pool and carry water away and in so doing mix it up with earth. For this reason, the water is usually very dirty. When I saw the small water source supplying two villages in the most difficult time of the year, I said god is a mystery. Imagine if this small water source were not there. Moreover, if it dries up one day, what becomes of these two villages? Surely, people would migrate to different villages.

A young man fetches water for me from Bella. Usually, I tell him to get very good water for me. When he returns, I ask, "Is the water good?" He replies, "Yes, it is very good water." I ask again, "Can I drink it?" He answers, "Yes, drink it, it is very good."

However, when I bring my bucket and he pours the water into it, the water is dirty and coloured as if a painter just mixed up colours to produce a picture of a semi desert landscape. In this landscape, part of it is green and parts of it a sandy desert. Inside one bucket, it seems the water has four colours. Colours that I cannot well determine or say. It is as brown as brown earth, dark as dark earth, white as white earth. When I leave this water to stand in the bucket through the night, by morning slimy mud particles have settled on the bottom and sides of the bucket. When I pour out this water, the original colour of the bucket is not seen until it is washed. If you look inside the drums the young men use in carrying water, you would see they do not wash these drums. Thick sticky matter falls in chunks with the water, and people see nothing wrong with this.

The human gut or colon resembles these unwashed containers. Faecal matter has been lining it for years. It causes us many diseases. When you do an enema and proper colon cleansing, maybe with warm water, this long stayed matter comes out, and many diseases are prevented. Nevertheless, people drink this muddy water without any purification. So far, I know only one aged woman in this village who purifies her drinking water with *eau de javel* or Clorox. Their systems are immune to the bad this water can cause. It does not make them sick compared to when a stranger drinks it. I found myself under the hot sun in places where I had no water with me. Although they encouraged me to drink, I did so very few times. Although they claim this water does not make them sick, there is no scientific evidence to prove this. Young men and women fall sick and sometimes die. Maybe poor living conditions generally, including poor water, contribute to this?

During the months of March, April and May where water is the scarcest, many children suffer from diarrhoea and many die too. They never associate this with poor drinking water. They only say it is like this every year or associate it with superstition.

There are three boreholes in Carrefour Poli. Therefore, if everything were normal, there would not be water problems. Unfortunately, nothing is normal. Before I arrived in the year 2008, the first two were already bad. They lacked repairs and so were not working. The last one, dug by the Chinese two years ago, is still good now. Nevertheless, it constantly gets bad and the villagers have to wait for the mechanic from Garoua, sometimes for weeks, to come and repair it. Even when this one is working, it cannot supply everyone with water. It takes time to pump the water out, and there is not enough to supply everyone for the whole day. When it gets deep into the dry season, it seems as if the water level falls and the amount of water we get slowly diminishes. A person has to wait there for many hours before getting a gallon of water, as the queue is long.

In addition, a maintenance fee is paid every month. Every grown up individual has to pay 500 francs ($1) a month and is entitled to eighty litres of water a day. If I say individual, it can stand for a family. For example, let's say a man has one wife and five children. It means the wife pays a dollar a month to get water for her, the husband and the children. If a man has two wives, it means those two women pay two dollars a month, because every woman is responsible for the water in her own household.

Not everyone in the village is able to afford such money for water. The poverty level is very high. I had a neighbour, a couple. They were migrating to another village in the month of April. I asked why they were moving. Another villager told me they lacked water. I said, "But there is water at the pump." The man laughed and said, "But you have to pay." I said, "But it is only 500 francs." He laughed again and told me that a dollar in my eyes might be small, but it is very difficult for the villagers to come up with it. He told me there are people in the village that do not make 1000 francs ($2) in two weeks. I wanted to know if this could be true. I thought this man was lying. I asked others around the village, and they admitted there was great poverty amongst some of the villagers. They affirmed there are people who for weeks and months touch only a few dollars with their hands.

There is poverty too in the southern part of Cameroon, but I think the level here is far greater. In southern Cameroon, in the rainy season, young men engage themselves seriously in farming. In the dry season, there is enough water in many places, so farmers are able to practice irrigation. Moreover, the rainy season is quite long, that is from March to October, which means people can spend the greater part of the year engaged in farming. Those who do not do farm work tap palm wine and sell it. Every region in the South has some activities to keep people busy and make some money. But here in the North, they get up in the morning, sit under trees, along every road and in front of their homes, and count cars as they pass by. If eyes could grow tired of seeing something and speak out, one day those eyes would tell them, "Please, I am tired of seeing cars; I want to see something else."

There is one zinc-roofed building in the school compound. When there is rainfall, even at midnight, the entire village comes out to place their basins and pots around the building to collect water. When I go to Garoua for the weekend, I always, unfailingly, return with a gallon of water that I will drink for that week. With the heat, we drink water like cows. Goats too drink a lot of water. On my arrival in the North, I did not know the connection between water and goats. One day, I stood two big buckets of water in front of my house and went away for a short time. On my return, those two buckets stood empty. I called the neighbours and asked who poured my water away. They told me that goats must have drunk the water. This was so alarming for me, because goats would not drink that much water in the South.

In any case, we suffer from lack of water in Carrefour Poli. The whole of northern Cameroon suffers from water problems. Probably some regions in the South suffer from this problem too, but it is not as bad as in the North. Even in some cities in Cameroon, there is the problem of water. Sometimes the inhabitants of Yaounde go without water, or even when there is water, the quality might not be good. The quality might be as bad as that which we have here in the North or even worse. There, authorities complain that the government built the water system for a lesser population.

The population of the cities has increased much over the years. This has taken the government by surprise? When they issue marriage certificates at the councils every day, what do they think is happening in the background? Men and women are producing. However, what did the town planners and politicians think when planning the smaller towns? People get married every day and children are born. Town and project planners may consult at the hospitals to know the number of children born each day. Even so, many are born at home and may not be counted. People migrate into towns every day. Town and project planners should consult the ministry of transport to know the number of people who migrate every day to the cities. Even so, many enter the cities on foot and may not be counted. Despite these facts that all of us know, they keep on with their own kind of planning and constructions. After twenty, thirty or forty years, they shall tell us again that roads, water systems, hospitals and schools were for lesser populations.

In Cameroon and African cities now, what can we do so that everyone gets water? It might mean that the whole mechanics of water supply system has to be redone. With this economic crisis, which is like a disease that afflicted the government, never to be cured, it is very difficult to break down the mechanics of the entire water system. The government does not have money and does not want to think about all these kinds of heavy projects. Please if you are thinking of this kind of project, keep it to yourself until when things become better in this country.

This does not mean, however, that the government is not carrying projects. There are bright new gigantic projects scattered all over the country. However, we must keep repairing the old ones until we shall reach a point where we start breaking down the old colonial time projects and rebuilding them. When that day shall come, every Cameroonian would have reason to smile, because many things would change for good.

Chapter 5

Government School Carrefour Poli and Peoples' Mentality towards Education

Teaching English in Government School Carrefour Poli is not an easy affair. Education in general in northern Cameroon is a challenge compared to southern Cameroon. Carrefour Poli is not an exception. Most young men and women have failed to attend school. They can neither speak nor understand French, let alone English. The level of illiteracy is high, but gradually we hope things will change. I went to the inspectorate of education in Lagdo. Arriving there, the office was closed. I saw a well-dressed man with a pen hanging in his shirt chest pocket walking up towards the office building. I thought he was a teacher. I asked him, "Please, are you a teacher, can you help me?" He replied, "No, sorry, I do not understand French." I was surprised at this reply. Then one day I was on the farm with my uncle who is an agroforestry scientist. One man in his forties came riding a motorbike. He was neatly dressed wearing dark sunshades with a good smile. He wanted to buy eucalyptus poles, but my uncle had to look for someone to translate between them, because that man could not understand nor speak a word in the French language.

Language can become a serious barrier in the entire North. Most of the northern people cannot go out of their region because of this problem. If you cannot communicate in at least one of the two official languages —French or English—, then you cannot travel, because nobody would understand you. When you are in the North, whether it is in

27

the market or on the road, everything is in the local languages. You must find a way to get your problem resolved when you face these language barriers, because to them, they have nothing to do, nothing can change.

Let us turn to Government School Carrefour Poli. This school has existed for over twelve years. It was first a community school, taken care of by the villagers. There is a single building comprising two classrooms built three years ago. The rest of the classrooms are made of sticks and grass. There are four government teachers, and the parents employ the rest of the teachers. The classrooms of grass and sticks do not last for more than one academic year. The villagers always build new classrooms in September, at the beginning of the new school year. The heavy downpours and storms destroy these classrooms. Classes stop when rain falls, because rain leaks into the classrooms. During heavy downpours, all the children in the school move to the brick wall and zinc roof classrooms. All classes have to stop, because all the pupils in the entire school crowd in there. There are few desks in these classrooms. The children sit on pieces of wood and stones. One day, a pupil lifted one of the stones in class three, and a viper emerged. Who knows if it could bite a child.

At school, pupils know very little French. Even the class six pupils' level in French is below average. This means that, because most of the pupils do not go beyond primary level, they will almost forget the little French they learnt at school when they leave. If these pupils are very poor in French, then how about the English language? Teaching English here is very frustrating. The teacher gets very tired and eventually lacks the zeal and motivation to persevere. This is because, no matter what you do, the pupils retain very little. To build them up to a level where they can express themselves even a little in English is a dream not easy to attain. The teacher can help them learn some words and know how to say the names of some objects and animals in English, but to build up their free flow of communication in English is a big problem. It is clear that when they leave school and fail to continue in secondary school, within a short time, the few English words they learnt will evaporate from their minds.

The student drop-out level is so high. Every year, you will see that the number of children who began school in September has dropped by the end of the first term. By the end of the second term, you see empty desks, wood, and stones everywhere in the classrooms. Then during the third term, about a month to the end of the school year, you will further observe that about one-third of the children in class six have dropped out. Class six children drop out a month before the date they have to write the First School Leaving Certificate (FSLC). This is the certificate that a pupil aims at, as he goes to school. But just a month to when they have to sit for the exams, he or she drops out. Are they afraid of the examination? I do not know. I asked and got tired and had no answer. Even if it is to leave school and marry, could they not wait until after the examinations?

When you meet children who dropped out and ask what happened, they always say, "No money." This surprises me, because the levy their parents chip in to employ teachers to help where government teachers are not enough is very small. The government has made education free, and if the parents have to pay 2000 francs ($4) per child for one academic year, I think that is very little. Because of four dollars a year, children drop out of school? Is it the level of poverty, or is there another hidden reason they do not want to say? When you ask some children why they dropped out, they just say,

"School is not going well." Maybe be the zeal to study is just not there? Many of the girls drop out between the ages of ten to fourteen years. When I do not see some of these small girls in class the next day, normally as a teacher I ask about them. The children just laugh. I press on for a reply, and suddenly one of the children will just burst out "married." Then follows laughter, ha ha ha, ho ho ho... everywhere in the class. Just last week, the last week of February 2013, one of the pupils of class four got married. When I asked repeatedly, this response came at last.

I know a man. He is about thirty years old. He had abandoned school many years ago and got a wife. Last year he decided and went back to school again. He wrote the "BEPC" (secondary school leaving certificate) and passed. When he passed the examination, he did not continue to the high school. He instead returned home. I asked him why he did not continue in the high school. He said he needed just the "BEPC" and no more. He is trying to write professional exams and work, and it is not easy to find work. Last year he got married to his second wife, which suggests he wanted just the secondary school certificate and that any more schooling was not his concern.

Even the male pupils drop out of school and get married. There was a boy in class six. He is tall, about one meter seventy-five centimetres. He has strong muscles with flat palms like those of a gorilla. His eyes are red, as if he just finished some bottles of beer. When I was teaching, he disturbed the class. I wanted to punish him. He stepped out of the classroom and told me that I would not punish him. After two weeks, he was no longer coming to school. I asked why. The children told me that he said it was for the good of the teachers that he stayed out of school. I asked what that meant. They said the boy told them, while in school, that he always resisted the temptation of giving the teachers a snake biting. To save the lives of the teachers, he therefore thought it wise to drop out of school. Our first aid box is empty, and there are no cars. Transporting an unconscious teacher on a motorbike to the health centre after a biting might be hopeless. It was indeed wise for this boy to drop out of school. He did so in December, when the first term holiday was approaching. When school re-opened in January for the second term, I told the children to ask him to come back to school. The pupils told me something that surprised me. They said he got married to his first wife and was even preparing to take in a second wife. Education was no longer for him, for he was busy raising his family. Thus not only girls but also boys drop out of school to marry.

This male pupil retired home without executing the evil that his dark side always tempted him to do. Violence by students on other students and teachers is common around the world. In the United States of America, an unhappy student might shed blood by unleashing a gun; people have been known to lose their lives in this way. When we were in the final class in the primary school, my giant classmate pushed his head between the legs of our round bellied teacher. With the teacher seated behind his neck, he lifted our teacher in an airplane flying style and threw him behind him. As our teacher fell, he knocked his head either on the desk or on the floor and wounded his forehead. The pupil wounded himself too. I was surprised at the behaviour of our teacher after this incident. All the pupils were shivering in class expecting a fight of the titans. Our teacher's house was nearby. He got up after the fall and went straight to his house. We did not know what he was going to do. If it was a long bearded and frightful traditional doctor, we might have said he was going home to bring his magic bag or wand, but it was a teacher. We feared if he returned with a gun, it might not be only the giant pupil but we too might be hurt. When he arrived back at school, we instead saw him with a bottle of iodine. He applied it on his wound and on that of the pupil too. The tension was over, and classes went on as usual.

There is no gun violence here in Cameroon, but if you are a teacher with men-pupils in class, you have to be careful because they have their own ways of handling troublesome teachers. A teacher relaxes by going around the village at night. He carries his small radio listening to the 7 pm news. Suddenly gravel pours on him like hailstones. How about the teacher whose body suddenly starts itching in the crowd or while dancing in the nightclub? Probably the pupils have sprayed a certain herb harvested in the forest on him. This herb is shaped like beans with hairy reddish skin. Students just have to rub the hairy skin into powder, and when the stubborn teacher is in the crowd, they spray it on him.

Leaving the malicious pupil, we turn now to some other kind of people spoiling the schoolgirls in our schools. Some men living around the village have very bad intentions. They are wicked, and if the children of Satan could live on earth, I am sure these people may be they. They have bad intentions for young schoolchildren. They will not rest until they have damaged and spoilt all these girls. They are in villages and cities all over Cameroon. Here is one example. A man is married to a young teenage girl, but this is not enough to quench the volcanic fire or the serpent fire rising in his spinal cord. He is a sex machine. He has discouraged young girls from going to school and has disvirgined them. He has spoilt so many girls. Unfortunately, or fortunately, things have not gone well for him recently. Maybe his magic failed, for he shall remember this period as the darkest period in his life as a sex maniac. He disvirgined one of the girls at night as he often does. The parents of the child discovered what was going on and handed the matter over to the law enforcement officials. The man was caught and locked up. A penalty was levied on him to pay to the girl's family. By the time I was writing this story, he was still in custody and the police would let him go only if that money was paid.

We all see how these little children have suffered in the hands of these matured men with their oversized donkey testicles, inflated beyond control after taking strong stimulants like "33" and Castel beer. When the teachers are in school suffering and doing their job properly to help these little girls grow more responsibly, these men are at home drawing plans to rupture all what the teachers have done. Thank god, to an extent, there exist the laws to bring them under control. These kinds of people are the number one enemies of the teachers.

We see again the Angel of peace dwell In Cameroon. Another man has caused this damage to the children of Muslims, and they also prefer to hand the matter over to the law to get it settled. In a different society outside Cameroon, the unfortunate Sharia law may show its head. Then those donkey testicles causing problems would be cut off. Let the law continue to be a place where we settle problems in Cameroon. Nobody, whether good or bad, is safe in a society that religious extremism has taken over. If this Angel of peace continues to watch over Cameroon, then in a long time to come, scholars all over the world will take particular interest in Cameroon. This shall happen when all or almost all the countries of the world have fought wars except Cameroon.

These scholars will flog to Cameroon in their numbers to learn, bite the tip of their pens, and sweat to study the art of peacekeeping. There will be Cameroonian ambassadors of peace installed in all countries of the world to see that there is no more fighting, no more wars around the world. This time shall be very interesting.

School absenteeism is really a big problem for village schools in the North. Schools re-open in September after the long vacation; our pupils return in October. After the celebration of youth day on the 11[th]of February, even if it falls on a Monday, children do not come to school for the rest of the week. They continue to celebrate youth day at home and only come to school the next week. I was in class this March 8th. I asked the pupils why the class was too scanty. They informed me that it was women's day, and children stay at home to celebrate. I thought what do children have to do with women's day, which is not even a public holiday. Luckily, this year, women's day falls on a Friday, so after spending the weekend celebrating, they may come to school on Monday; if not, they might continue celebrating women's day at home for the rest of the week. Parents have a big role to play in the education of children. Teachers encourage children to come to school. However, when the children are at home, it is the role of the parents to motivate their children to return to school. The teacher cannot go to homes to bring children to school. The church may tell us there is a saint, who went from home to home to bring children to school, so we might start to invoke him.

With the coming of the rains, the children are also absent from school. In a year where the rains come early, that is in May, children abandon school and go to the farms. In the South, the rains begin in March and go through October and sometimes November. Because the rain begins late in the North and goes into October, the farming season is short, and people want to seize the opportunity to work the land. In the month of May, Mr. Goyoko, the headmaster, who is now retired, sits under a tree in the schoolyard with piles of papers before him. There is no office for him; he sits under a tree in the schoolyard. The tree is his canopy and shades him from the sun. He moves his table and chair several times a day as the earth rotates. During the breaks, we the teachers leave our classes and sit on the stones around this tree, with Mr. Goyoko in the centre. This reminds me of the old folk stories of times past, when children sat around mothers and waited for the food to be ready. They would feel the healing warmth of the fire and of good stories. This also reminds me of those days where novices sat around their long-bearded masters, receiving mouth-to-ear initiations. Unfortunately, this tree was brought down in one of the storms.

Mr. Goyoko puts on his reading glasses. He takes his time and completes the school records. Age is weighing on him. He hopes to retire soon. He takes about a week to fill out documents that a young teacher may take just a few hours complete. However, he likes his job; he is conscientious and wants to do the work alone and perfectly. The other young headmasters who came after him are lazy and fear to work. They always call on other teachers to come and help them fill in the records.

As Mr. Goyoko works, he feels a kind of cool breeze brush past his skin. It is different; it is not the normal everyday breeze that usually passes. He knows it is already May, and the rains may fall. He stands up and lifts his head with his grey hair glittering in the sun. He observes the weather. His experience of almost sixty years of age tells him there might be rain. He does not need weather observation instruments. He moves from class to class and instructs the teachers to give the sixth sequence examinations: "Please, let the children write the sixth sequence examination, if it rains, all the children will go to the farms." He warns that if the rainfalls when any teacher has not yet given his examination, it concerns that teacher alone. He has done his job in alerting the teachers to give the examinations. When he gives this announcement, dare not take it as a joke and fail to give the examination. When that first rainfalls, go to school. You, the teacher, will sit there alone looking at empty desks, stones or wood, depending on what the children sat on. Parents will even pass in the school compound before you with their children and go to the farms. That examination is the teacher's problem and no longer their problem.

Traditional circumscription causes some boys to be absent from school. This takes place in the forest, and the children have to live there for at least one month. We will devote one chapter ahead to talk about this ceremony.

I sometimes wonder whether the education we try to share with those who come to school passes through them. In many ways, I doubt it. Many children sit in class looking at the teacher, without doing the work you have given to them. The commonplace reasons are: there is no pen, no pencil, no chalk and no book. Then what is the purpose of coming to school? It is like this every day, and you the teacher wonder what to do. I once gave two pens —a blue and red pen— to a child that had none. After two weeks, the father met me on the road and said the pens were missing and that I should provide more. Since this 2012/2013 academic year began, I have not seen that particular child in school. Maybe he has dropped out of school and maybe that is it for his education, or maybe you will see him again in school next year. Nobody can predict the pupils.

Even during examinations, pupils that do not have pens sit and fold their arms. They do seem worried, as they tell the teacher while smiling that they do not have pens. That examination is the teacher's problem and not the pupils' problem. After all, there is collective promotion. This is an education policy to promote all the children to the next class. Hierarchy has instructed us, the teachers, and we just have to follow. The entire class is a team. Individual abilities merge into the team, and the herd moves together to the next class. With teamwork, life is so easy, life is good, and there is no need for worries. Every child is sure to go to the next class, even if they fail to meet the required standards. Whether their heads are calabashes of knowledge or water, they are going to the next class.

When classes are going on, there are numerous distractions and disturbances. A snake hiding under a stone may come out, and that is another serious problem. Most of the desks that were available are now broken pieces of wood. The children pile them up and sit on them. A loud noise in class might mean those piled pieces of wood or timbers have collapsed and pupils' have to arrange them back.

However, in every class, as an English teacher, you encounter a few pupils who try to do well in English. If they continue in the same spirit, I am sure they will be very good in English as they advance.

Failure of education in the North comes from all directions. Even the serious pupils are harmed, sometimes by the headmasters and the teachers. How about the children who paid their final examination fees, and the headmaster melted with the money? The headmaster becomes invisible and, despite all searches, is not found.

On the day of the examination, children can be seriously disturbed. To conclude negotiations to let them write, the chief examiners had to send the children out several times. Most of the intelligent pupils who failed claimed that it was these interruptions and lack of peace that made them fail. Time was cut short as they stayed outside the examination hall for some time. Many things went wrong, and normally people will not do well while writing examinations under tension.

How about the teacher, while carrying pupils' examination slips and birth certificates, drank the locally brewed beer and forgot where he kept these documents? This can lead to serious confusion. One day, a pupil brought the documents forward, saying that the teacher gave them to her for safekeeping. Because she did not know how important or urgent those documents were, she kept them to bring them when it was convenient for her, as the teacher did not also ask. Everything is in limbo. We are in limbo.

In any case, the government is trying its best to encourage education in Carrefour Poli and the "Grand North" as a whole. Nevertheless, this takes time. The changes are slow, but the good news is that there are changes. There are many primary, secondary, and high schools and technical schools everywhere. Many young boys and girls of the northern villages go to secondary schools. Although many fall out before the final years of high school, many go on to university. This is a good change. The mentality of the people slowly changes, and they are more conscious that both boys and girls have to go to school. So everything is moving in a positive direction.

Chapter 6
The People and their Livelihood

There is hunger. Surely, Jesus Christ was god in human flesh. If not so, he would not have been able to resist Satan's temptation, in such hunger, from turning sand and stones into bread. If many of us had such an opportunity, we would not only want bread but all kinds of delicious food. Moreover, humans eat a lot of food every day around the world. If we had such powers, we would lack sand and stones to build because humans would convert all into food. Unfortunately, those powers are not common; we have to work for our food. The people of the North and Cameroon in general work so hard for their daily bread.

The farming season in the North in general and in Carrefour Poli in particular is very short. The rains come in June and go away in September or there may be one or two rains in October. Sometimes in a lucky or good year, the rains begin in the month of May. You have to be smart, ready and swift to plough and plant in May. Get your seeds and everything ready because two rains might fall in May or early June, and the next rainfall is only after a month. Those who were ready should have planted when the first two to four rains fell. These are the lucky ones, for they might end up being the ones to harvest for that year. Generally, however, the mass of the population plants in June, and if June passes and you have not yet planted corn and sorghum, you have to fight and catch up with time. You have to do everything possible to plant before mid-July.

The people of northern Cameroon plant mostly groundnut, because it does not need fertilizers to do well.

Each family should have enough to sell, eat and preserve seeds for the next farming season. They also cultivate many varieties of sorghum, which is the basic foodstuff for almost all families in northern Cameroon.

Corn too is very important as people eat "fufu cornmeal" two or three times a day. When those of us from the South heard that Northerners eat "fufu corn" every day, we disbelieved this but it is actually true. All three meals of the day can be "fufu cornmeal," made from corn or sorghum. People may change the accompanying soup a few times, but not very much. When I arrived in Carrefour Poli, for the first month I did not have my own house. I lived with one of the families. In the morning, there was a bit of tea and bread. In the afternoon, there was "fufu cornmeal." This was the routine meal for the one month I lived with this family.

Unfortunately, few people are able to cultivate corn. They have to buy maize in small bowls from the market to consume. Most people cannot afford the high cost of cultivating corn. Without the application of inorganic fertilizers, corn does not do well in the farms. These fertilizers are very expensive. As a whole, to cultivate an acre of corn farm, the farmer needs 250 000 francs ($500). This amount should be able to move an acre of corn farm from plough to harvest. Most of the people cannot afford this sum of money; in short very few people can. As a result, a few still grow corn, but because the application of fertilizer is not enough, the yields are poor. In a farm that does well, the yields from an acre of corn can be between three and four tons.

If well done, farm yields in corn and groundnut are far better here. In the South, the yields might be less. Here villagers work in their farms with the children, relatives and friends. They understand how to go about this and do not pay much for labour.

They also cultivate cotton with the help of SODECOTON (*Société de développement du coton*). SODECOTON gives the farm inputs like fertilizers, herbicide and insecticide. At the end of the farming season, the company deducts the money from the sum they have to pay to the farmers. The farmers form associations that in turn have delegates who represent them at SODECOTON. However, as it is with human nature, the delegates have failed the villagers.

I know one of the delegates who ran away with farmers' dues up to 400 000 francs ($800). He collected fertilizers from SODECOTON. Instead of handing them over to the farmers, he sold them and confiscated the money. When I heard about this, I asked if his home could be sold to recover the money. The village people around me laughed. I asked why. They told me that nobody would even buy the man's home for 50 000 francs ($100). By this time, I was still new in the North. I did not yet know that their village homes cost almost nothing. Their homes are almost valueless. In the South, the value of homes and land are high. We have many fruit trees and palm trees of high value. In addition, homes in the South are roofed with corrugated sheets with good value. Here in the North, the value of land is extremely cheap. Families have no fruit trees at home. They build their houses with earth (mud), sticks and grass. These are all gifts that the people collect freely. They use these three materials to build their houses. Therefore, nobody could buy this man's home even for 20 000 francs ($40).

When you arrive in the North, be very careful listening to the people as they tell you about the good harvest they get from every acre of land they plough. Use your money wisely, so as not to be the looser in the end. When I arrived, they told me all these stories of good harvest. I was excited and thought I would be a very successful farmer in the North. I went ahead and borrowed money from my micro finance bank. I invested this money in a few acres of land. I cultivated corn, cowpea, Roselle (*folere* in a local language and hibiscus in English), soya beans and groundnut. I gathered all my harvest from the farm in November and December. I sent it to a relative in the South to sell it for higher prices. This relative lives in Bafoussam in western Cameroon. From the day the goods arrived, his phone number no longer went through. It was clear that he sat and luck came to him. He sold all the goods and vanished with the money. The police arrested him later, but he was as dry as a desert. He was very poor, wretched; his lips were dry and cracked like the Sahara desert. It was clear he lacked innutrition and in bodily fluids. The police kept him for a few days but became frightened. His eyes were sunken like in the "zombie" films. His spinal cord began to form a "C" and started to resemble the shape of a dry dead lizard or the back of a living tortoise. The police could not support this and asked for his immediate release, which I accepted. If the law of karma or cause and effect is true, then he has scores to settle with me in this lifetime or in another incarnation.

That is not the end of the story for me. The money I borrowed from the micro finance bank was causing me problems. It was my first time to borrow money from a bank, and I did not know how banks work. These micro finance banks are into a "shylock" kind of business. They get cut throat interest from the money they lend to customers. They do very good advertisements and attract you to join them. We are happy to join, as we see them as very promising. They flash us with attractive conditions for loans. Then you go on, get their money and start regretting it almost immediately.

The banks hide something from you. They do not let you know the interest rate and many other things. They cannot reveal everything. You get the money and start to complain about dirty tactics and stealing. They reply that "you signed and got the money." They slash your money without pity. When you want to break off the unholy marriage, they will not let you go. The marriage certificate is the invisible chain they have tied around your neck and their waist. To break the marriage, you are attempting to pull the chain. You pull the chain, your neck pains. Their waists are already accustomed to the everyday pulling. They do not feel the pains.

Just like a chronic disease that ate up the internal organs of the marathon runner until he instantly dropped dead, so too the interiors of the micro-finance institutions in Cameroon are rotten. That is why today we hear that "all-star" micro- finance has collapsed, and tomorrow we hear that "bright star" micro finance has collapsed as well. The chronic disease is killing the micro-finance banks one after another. Sudden death all the time, and the doctor (government) has not yet found the antidote. At their death, they drag unfortunate ones with them into the grave. Did Mr. Tom's urgent surgery not fail because he lost all his savings? Did the children of Mr. Jonathan not fail to enter university because he lost all his savings? The list is very long. A person saves money today and falls sick after a week. He goes to the same building where he saved the money. He sees something very different. People sit everywhere drinking beer, and the music is roaring as if a Chinese dragon has awakened after five thousand years of sleep. He steps in despite the confusion and says, "I want to see the bank manager." Then comes the reply of: "Here we have but a bar manager." He goes home weeping because he understands his hard earned money is gone.

Well, that small reflection was for those who want to borrow money from the micro-finance banks and invest in the farms; they should think twice.

Though farming is a source for livelihood, this does not mean that most young men really work hard. Most are lazy. They do not go to the farms. When you call them up for even the smallest work, they tax you high, and when you are unable to pay, they prefer to sit by the roadside doing nothing. They claim to be farmers, but very few of them own machetes, hoes and farm tools in general. When you hire them for farm work, you have to provide them with farm tools because most of them do not have any.

Some of the people of Carrefour Poli do wood carving or woodwork. They carve mortars and stools, stand them along the Garoua-Ngaoundere main road and sell them to travellers. They have felled trees for more than forty years, and the trees are fewer. The desert is approaching. One day, I told the master wood carver to choose a piece of land and plant trees there. I say choose a piece of land because, all land is almost free. It is not very difficult to acquire even large piece of land. He told me that he does not have the time to plant trees. He told me there are always trees in the forest. I told him that there are trees but fewer than before. I asked him to compare the tree density when he began woodwork about twenty or twenty-five years ago to the current situation. He acknowledged that the trees are fewer in number. He walks long distances to find trees to cut, unlike twenty years ago. Despite acknowledging that there are fewer trees, he still said he was not going to plant any.

Preserving things for future generations does not seem to be of concern. Planting trees means planning for the future generation, for "my children's" future, but why worry about this when there is god? God plans for the future and not man. A man once carried me on a motorbike. I told him to reduce his high speed. I was surprised when he asked, "Do you not have a child?" I asked him what a child has to do with speeding on a motorbike. He said, "People who do not yet have children are afraid to die." I asked, "And if you have children and then they die, who takes care of the children?" He replied, "God takes care of the children." Thus, no need planning for the future generation. Our heads and brains are for what? We should not think and make better decisions, just wait for god to do everything?

One day I saw fresh red blood oozing out of the big toe of the master wood carver. I asked him what happened. He told me that the forestry people controlling the trees and woodcutting came around. As he ran away carrying his mortars and stools, he cracked his big toe against a stone. He said if he did not run with his carvings, these forestry people would seize them all. Shortly thereafter, the forestry people were no longer seizing woodworks. They began receiving 100 francs for every carved object. Is this tax collection or the preservation of the forest? Carvers are paying 100 francs for every piece of woodwork, but the trees are disappearing. The Sahara desert is approaching, getting a few kilometres closer every year. All the water in Lake Chad is gone, and trees keep disappearing. After all, 100 francs five times makes a dollar, which is equal to a bottle of beer to quench one's thirst in the Sahara desert.

This problem of surveying and preserving resources is a big problem. A species of fish here in the North is almost extinct. When mature, the fish is about six or seven centimetres long. However, farmers catch this fish when it is still tiny, just about two centimetres long. The government wants to protect this fish species. One day, I was on the bus going to Garoua. A man was standing together with the police at the police checkpoint. This man was wearing a white garment like the one Jesus used to wear in very powerful operations. Alternatively, we may say a white robe like the one a most powerful surgeon has on, ready to do surgery on an important statesman. Our bus stopped. This man touched a bag on the carriage of the bus and said, "This is the fish! Who owns this bag?" The destroyer of a protected species, a man in his fifties, was sitting in the front of the bus with a carefree attitude, chewing kola nuts. The protector of species asked repeatedly until the destroyer of species owned up. As he owned up, we saw him dipping his hand into the pocket of his good for nothing jacket. He removed something and pressed it into the man's palm. He took it, then opened and surveyed his palm. We saw how this man protested, "No, this is too small, give at least 200 francs!" The destroyer of resources had pressed 100 francs into his palm; he hesitated but at last added another 100 francs, which made 200 francs. This is not up to half a dollar, and the natural resources are gone. If two more destroyers of resources pass, the protector would have at least a dollar for his bottle of beer.

One other activity of livelihood for the people of Carrefour Poli in the North and the entire country is bike riding. Because there are no taxis in the North, bike riding is a lucrative activity. Bikes are the main mode of transport within towns and the outskirts of towns. In Carrefour Poli, most young boys are involved in this business. Sometimes boys in their teens drop out of school for motorbike riding. They hire the bikes and pay the owner about 3000 francs ($6) a day, and the rest of the money they earn is theirs. It is a risky profession for both the driver and the passengers. They carry so many people on these bikes, at times up to five people. They also go at high speeds and without headlamps at night. There are fatal consequences. Many die from motorbike accidents. Many people become physically handicapped as a result of motorbike accidents. People have broken legs and arms that never completely healed.

In 2009, there was one of these fatal accidents near LANAVET, the national veterinary laboratory, on the road to Garoua. Five people were returning from the market on a motorbike at 7 pm; it was already dark. The bike had no headlamp. Because there were five people on the bike, the driver was sitting on the petrol tank itself. His thighs were almost on the steering wheel. A heavy truck approached from the opposite direction. The bike plunged into a pothole in the middle of the road. Because the driver was sitting on the steering wheel, it was difficult for him to regain control. They went face to face with the heavy truck. You can imagine what this means. Imagine Mike Tyson fighting with a baby. What do we expect? A disaster of course. All five people died on that spot. Their flesh and body parts were scattered all over. If people could reach heaven or hell depending on how they die, they would have taken a fraction of a second to be there. After searching their pockets, no identification papers were found. Nobody knew where they came from. Following the culture of the northern people, they do not keep the dead for long. Their scattered bodies were buried on the spot almost immediately. We all wonder where their families thought they went to from the market. When I go around, I restrict motorbike riders from carrying more than two passengers. Moreover, when they go too fast, I ask them to slow down.

Many boys and men earn their living by riding these bikes. The rate of unemployment is so high. One day a man came from Kribi and said he wanted young men to go to Kribi and work. He promised to pay each of them 100 000 francs ($200) a month. Almost all the young men of Carrefour Poli went with him, but within a month, they began returning one by one until all of them returned. The fruitful future they hoped for in Kribi turned out to be a faulty adventure.

Some of the women do a few things like frying and selling gateaux (small cakes), fish and sweet potato. These women also brew and sell the local beer called "bily bily." A majority of the people drink this local beer because it is cheap and affordable. Some women sell a locally brewed wine call "dangflang." The people drink "bily bily" and "dangflang" in heavy amounts. Nobody would be contented without these two drinks. Life would never be normal without them.

There is another wine simply called "gas." "Gas" is very dangerous. You have to dilute it very well with water before drinking it. One day in a small market in Sanguere Paul, 10 kilometres from Garoua town, a man in his twenties died from this drink. How did it happen? In the evening, a seller of this drink stepped away from his market stall for a while. This man knew fully well it was undiluted gas in the bottle in the stall. Maybe he was already drunk from previous drinks. Nevertheless, the truth is that he took that bottle of undiluted "gas" and drank from it. He collapsed immediately. His relatives carried him home, and he died in less than ten minutes. He left behind a pregnant wife and two children. We cannot tolerate that kind of careless death or suicide. Everything is limbo. We are in limbo.

Life goes this way for the people of Carrefour Poli and Northerners in general. There is mass poverty, but when it is the harvesting season, people sell groundnut, and all the drinking places are full. Small markets under big trees sell "bily bily," "dangflang," "odongtong," "gas", and other local drinks. People are happy. Life goes on. We wait for when the last breath will come.

Chapter 7

The People, Health Care and Nutrition

There is a health post at Gouna, precisely four kilometres from Carrefour Poli. However, most people hardly go to this health post or to the hospital for any ailment. Whether it is malaria, typhoid fever or whatever the name, they do not go to the hospital. Many times, you hear that this or that person died. If you ask if he or she was sick, you will hear there was just a small illness of one or two days, then the person died. They think a one or two day illness is not enough to kill a person. They fail to realize that a person already weakened by years of poor nutrition could be killed by one or two days of malaria. However, this could be treated if medical attention were sought. But because they do not go to hospital, internal illnesses are eating them up. They think about the hospital when they see a person lying sick in bed, when the disease is already chronic and difficult to cure. When the disease finally takes away the life of the diseased, they attribute the death to demons, or ill luck, or a family vendetta.

The water source here in Carrefour Poli and the North in general is not good. This bad water should cause many diseases. However, the people never think of this as a factor that causes diseases. Their diet is imbalance. They eat "fufu corn" every day in all three meals. This dish lacks most of the healthy nutrients to help them resist diseases. People who live on a balanced diet should be able to resist disease better. If they could vary the "fufu corn soup" as much as possible, it might be different. They cultivate and have more groundnut

51

than we have in the South. Groundnut is a good protein source, but they fail to use it regularly for their soup. They sell almost the entire groundnut harvest from the farms. In the South of Cameroon, we have many varieties of foodstuff, and we vary our soup each time we eat. We make our soup with groundnut, egusi (pumpkin seeds), soya beans and an uncountable variety of green leafy and root vegetables. Foodstuff in the South is much more affordable. In the cities of the North, varieties of foodstuff are available occasionally in the market. However, it is too expensive for the average person. In Carrefour Poli, people have to live on maize and sorghum. That is what is available, and the people do not have another choice.

An herb called "kinkeliba" grows wild on farms and in the hills here. Almost all households harvest this plant during the rainy season. They eat some and dry and store the rest for the dry season. They use the leaves of this herb to make soup to go with "fufu corn." I lived with a friend for one week and saw how he prepared this soup. He gets up very early every morning and prepares "fufu corn." After making the "fufu," he boils about two glasses of water and puts about one or two tablespoons of the powdered herb into the boiled water. He adds salt and stirs. It gets slippery like okro. That is all. The soup is ready in less than five minutes. He eats this meal every day and starts drinking "bily bily" and all the locally made wines day after day. This is how most people here eat throughout the year.

With this kind of poor diet, when a person falls sick, without any medical care, he or she may not survive. When you sit with people, you see how they mix whisky into "bily bily" and drink it. You see how a young man rubs kola nuts in Mentholatum and eats them. What is the chemistry of all these mixtures inside the human body and physiology? With all these kinds of mixtures, potentially toxic, on a daily basis, what kind of lifespan do we expect? You see how young men sniff "snuff" into their heads; everywhere they go, you see them holding small cups of snuff. In the South, I see only old people taking "snuff." I have a friend. When he is visiting me, I always hide my onions, otherwise he would eat them all up. When he grabs one big onion, he does not need a knife; he bites it about four times, eats it and sweats. I sit and watch, ashamed to say, "Please stop eating my onion." One big onion is gone and if I am not lucky, the second will follow. It is useless to tell him that raw onion eaten heavily and frequently may generate internal damp heat leading to disease. This would fall on deaf ears. This was in the beginning when I arrived here in Carrefour Poli. I now know him as an expert onion eater, thus when I hear his voice calling "Mr. John, Mr. John," I gather all my onions and allow only one to be exposed.

When you ask them why they do not vary their food, they say, their stomach stays hollow when they eat other food. They say it is like a big hole, gap or empty space in their belly when they eat other foodstuffs like beans, potatoes or rice. As soon as they eat "fufu corn," this empty space vanishes. Even when they have rice, after cooking it, they use a stick to turn and mix it to form a paste, like that of "fufu corn."

Because there are many snakes in the environs of Carrefour Poli, snakebites are common. People do not go to the hospital to treat these bites. They stay at home with the wound. At night, most of them go without shoes. Most of the snakebites are on the feet. They go around at night without torches. They mostly wear slippers. As they go around, they step on these snakes. A snake will never spare you when you step on it. Therefore, the snakes are defending themselves by biting. Most of the time, people do not realize on the spot that they have been bitten by a snake. They realize it when they have arrived home and feel pain on a foot. They then look and see blood. Yet after noticing this, they stay at home with it. By some grace, they get well at last or the unlucky ones may die.

The next mystery is that almost all the women give birth at home. A man told me that whenever his wife is labouring to give birth, according to his tribe's custom, he leaves his wife alone. He does not stay near her. He leaves the room and stays outside. He does not call for the neighbours or any other person to come and assist his wife. He leaves his wife to herself to deliver the baby. He stays outside, not too far from the house. The wife labours alone in the house. He stays outside unafraid. He lifts his ears up like those of a rabbit and listens. When he hears the cry of a baby, he rushes in and receives the child. I asked him, as his wife is alone, if there are some unforeseen problems, how does it work out? He told me that it is not in all cases that women stay alone to give birth. He said in many cases, family, relatives and neighbours attend to the women. However, he acknowledges that many problems do occur in some cases for the following reasons.

i) Difficult delivery is most often the work of demons or the handiwork of Satan. He said demons and Satan are very wicked and at times do not want the baby to be delivered. He said there are wicked spirits or demons that have been hovering behind the woman even before she got married. These evil spirits and demons want the most favourable time to trap the woman and that is during childbirth. He offered a solution to this problem. He said the family should slaughter a big cock and offer it as a sacrifice to the demon and thereafter, the woman can give birth. He told me that those evil spirits want blood. Once the evil spirit inhales the fowl's blood, s/he allows the woman to deliver.

This story may be true or not, I do not know, but one day early last year we were in school. News spread quickly around the village about a couple in the farms. As they worked, their baby lay in a shady place under a tree. After a while, they went to carry their baby away but did not see the child. They searched in the farms around and in the entire village but did not find the child. They reported this to the police at Lagdo, and their search was futile too. The couple decided to consult a fortune-teller. The fortune-teller told them to look for a live cock and tie it in the farm where the child was taken. They did as instructed and went home. They went back to the farms at 4 am the next morning and found the child there. The fortune-teller said the demon wanted blood and by taking the cock for its blood, he had to hand the child back. When we hear and see these kinds of things, it is left for everyone to draw his or her own conclusions. After this story of bloodthirsty demons, let us go back to the reasons for difficult deliveries.

ii) The second reason for difficult deliveries as told by this man connects to the sins of the woman giving birth. This man said these sins might be deeply rooted, since before marriage, or committed after marriage. The sins committed before marriage might mean that this woman committed fornication with a male blood relative of hers while she was young. This is a terrible sin. It will lead to difficult delivery when she eventually gets married. The sins committed after or during marriage have to do with adultery. This means a woman has been having sexual relationship with someone or some others, other than her husband. He said this too is a terrible sin, an unforgivable sin which also leads to difficult delivery.

This philosopher and master of difficult delivery, attributes all faults to the woman. The man is an island and has no blame. Man is safe and has no sins. However, he said there was a solution for these sins, for god is so kind. The solution for these two problems is simple; the woman should name the male relative she committed fornication with. In the case of adultery, she should name the man or the men she has been committing adultery with. With these confessions, she would deliver the baby, this philosopher assured me. Confessions done and the woman gives birth. What are the implications of all this in the village? Will there be a fight between the woman's husband and these men who have been secretly cheating on him? Will the woman come to shame? Will the man divorce his wife? These are some of the unanswered questions.

iii) Mr. Philosopher went on with the last reason that causes difficult deliveries. This is when in polygamy, another mate hates the mate who is delivering. With such hatred, the child is blocked in the womb. The solution for this problem is that the wicked mate is asked to let go of her anger or wickedness so that the child is delivered.

However, he said, sometimes the woman may labour for about two days without giving birth. This would mean that the woman's pathway for the baby to pass through is small. In this case, the woman would be carried to the hospital. The medical doctor would increase the woman's pathway and bring forth the child. For him, this is almost the only reason that can cause a woman not to deliver. He said, without the hand of Satan and demons, without sins, the woman will normally deliver her baby without problems.

There is frequent diarrhoea and dysentery amongst people in the North. I always hear they blame this on bad "bily bily" that they drank somewhere. I have never heard them blame bad water or any other thing for being the cause of these diseases. They always buy a few tablets of Flagyl along the road, take them, and soon feel better, according to their standards. God has made the human system to be able to heal itself whenever there is disharmony, with or without medicine. The system can heal itself and adjust without medicine by observing simple natural rules, if we are aware of them. Just by eating the right food, drinking pure or boiled water, taking rehydration solution when necessary, purging the system by proper eating and fasting, all these will go a long way to restore our organism to proper functioning when an illness occurs.

Most of the people do not have toilets. They deposit everything in the grass behind the houses. They do not care and are never ashamed. When you pass by, you see them hovering in the bushes or in the grass. There was a man; unfortunately, he is of late now. I do not know if he was mentally all right or not. What I know is that he always sang as he passed near my house into the grass behind to deposit the thing. Each time, on his return, he would not only sing, he would sing and dance while jogging. Maybe he never danced when going because he felt the strong urge to pass out the thing.

This week you hear that a young man dies; next week another dies. I am sure lack of proper nutrition and medical care are major causes of death amongst the youth, premature greying of hair and ageing. Everything is in limbo. We are in limbo.

Chapter 8

Marriage and the Family

As in almost all of Africa, family sizes are usually large. A single man has many wives and children, thus the majority of the population belongs to polygamous homes. So too in Carrefour Poli and the North as a whole, the trend is not different. Nevertheless, in recent years, there is a difference in marriage trends between the Northerners and the Southerners. In the southern part of the country, many young men are trying to shift from polygamous marriages to monogamy. In the North, most people still marry or hope to take in the second, third and even fourth wife. In southern Cameroon, young men are not only intending to stay with a single wife, but they are also trying to reduce the number of children per family. When our parents and grandparents watch this new trend, it is very strange to them and they are not satisfied with it. They would have loved to see every male child with at least two wives and as many children as possible.

In the past, a man who had many wives was seen as the strongest around the village. A man with many wives and children was the weightiest person in the society. The wives of my paternal grandfather that I knew or heard of are eight, and I am sure that was not all; some that I did not know must have died or divorced. The wives of my maternal grandfather whom I knew or heard of are six, while some must have died or divorced that I did not know. Looking at the generation of our grandparents, those with two or three wives were just somewhere around the middle. There were men with up to twenty or more wives and still many having between six and ten. For the chiefs, we cannot count their wives. The wives of a chief could make a small village. At that time, the chief did not have to negotiate with a young girl nor with her parents before marrying her. If the nobles spotted a young girl good for the chief, they had to forcefully make her wear a special bangle around her wrist, maybe in the marketplace, and automatically, she becomes the chief's wife. The young, poor girl could not do anything about this. In recent years, thank god this tradition is gone. Even if it still exists today, there would be a lot of resistance to it. People are more conscious of what they want for their female children, than to become the thirtieth wife of a chief. In those days, if a father opposed, he would surely suffer heavily for standing against the chief. Maybe he would be excommunicated from the village. Maybe all his property would be seized.

Our grandparents, parents and the chiefs needed these populous homes, because they had coffee, banana plantations and raffia bushes. If a man was powerful, all the work done in his plantations went on successfully without employing outside forces. The children were the labour force. An ambitious man hoping to operate on many acres of land had to marry many women to give him the children. Education was not a priority for the children. It is in recent times, since the coming of the white man (colonization), that education became popular. Before then, as children grew, the girls were handed over for marriage and the boys worked in the farms.

As we said, the marriage trend here in the North may not be changing much. The men in Carrefour Poli and the North in general still continue to marry many wives. Most men are polygamist. However, there are some men with one wife. Nevertheless, just because a man lives with just one wife, that does not mean he will live all his life that way. Maybe he is still preparing himself to take in the second wife, or some other things may stand in his way preventing him from further marriages. Their intention here is to take in as many wives as possible. It is good to wait until a person dies before we conclude he is a monogamist. Even at age sixty and above, men continue to take in new wives. The men do not spend much money before and after marriage. The women deliver at home. They do not spend much money in educating the children. When they are sick, god is expected to take care of them.

They do not spend much money in constructing houses. The climate is very hot, so most of the time they can sleep in the yard on their mats. Even to build their houses, as I mentioned before, it costs almost nothing. They build only single room houses and not apartments. They make about three hundred bricks to make a single room house. They build the room by themselves. They thatch the roof with grass. The parents do all this work with the children, relatives and friends. When the rooms are complete, some of them allow the doors to be open without door covers. On the other hand, they may buy a door made of a sheet of zinc in the market for 5000 francs ($10). That might be all they have spent in building that room. Or else, somebody who does not fit a door onto his house spends completely nothing for that room. They build the rooms without windows, or they might put a window of thirty square centimetres. Most of the windows do not have window covers, or they prepare and fit something there that they do not need to buy. Most of the rooms do not last for many years. This is because the heavy rains soon penetrate the grass roofs destroying the walls of the house. They have to redo the thatched roofs after every two or three years. Despite all the renewal, if there is no luck, the rooms still end up collapsing. They do not regret the collapse of the buildings. After all, it cost them nothing. They just have to build another one. Nothing is long lasting. You see that by the ease with which they construct their houses. Without spending financially, they can have as many children as possible. They are not worried where children would live; they can live anywhere, even in the yard.

Marriage here is very simple. A person gets married today; tomorrow they are divorced. A woman would have one child with the first husband. Divorced, she marries the second husband and has one or two children. There is a vicious circle. Marry, give birth, divorce. This vicious circle continues until old age or death gets hold of her. Divorce is something very normal. It is as if everybody already knows it has to be that way. When the women leave the first marriage, they leave the children behind. As they leave the second marriage, they still leave the children behind, and it continues this way. The divorce rate is not easy. Some women come to the world to run this race. Unfortunately, women do not win medals for divorce. However, this does not mean there are no stable marriages; there are still many that are very stable.

For most young girls, their first marriage is often between the ages of twelve and sixteen, except for the few who attend secondary school. For the boys, they marry early too. Most of the boys get married either before the age of twenty or in their early twenties. A stable job or financial security is not a condition for marriage. You need to have your room, which cost nothing to construct, and a mat on the floor as your bed. Nevertheless, this does not mean that some of them do not have beds. Some have beds made of cane from the forest. A bed made of cane costs 3000 francs ($6). I have mine, however, I put a mattress on it. Most of the villagers would have just a mat on it, which is not as comfortable.

When the wife comes, she will start struggling to obtain maize to prepare the "fufu corn." The man starts making his children. The man knows there is no limit for child making. Only the sky is the limit. Making as many children as possible is good, because there is always the fear that some of the children may die. Some may die. Some must still survive, and those are the ones that shall bury the father at his death. Because the father is fully conscious of this, he does not joke if it comes to making children. When the first wife is tired, the second will continue. This may continue up to the fourth wife. Only god can decide when one may stop taking in new wives. The woman gets tired of bringing forth children, but the man does not get tired. My paternal grandfather took in a new wife in his seventies though he died at age one hundred and fifteen. Man is lucky; he can even marry again at the age of one hundred. It is never late; only the grave would stop a man from this wonderful ambition.

When a young couple marries, they breathlessly await their first child. Will the unborn child be a boy or girl? If it is a girl, there are big celebrations that can last even for months. They believe that female children bring in wealth and luck. The family takes good care of the woman. She does not have to work. She has to rest, and her food is well prepared.

This is contrary to the male first born. The man does not see well with this. There is not much joy. This is because the male child would be an unmistakable rival to the father. That is why, when the male child grows up to around the age of eighteen or twenty, the father helps him build his own home at a good distance from his. This new-born male child should be the father's rival in eighteen or twenty years to come. By the time this child is eighteen, he may have the same age or even be older than the father's third or fourth wife. That is where the danger is. This is a great risk, which no father wants to take. This child at eighteen is more handsome and vigorous than the fifty year old father. The father cannot underestimate the danger resulting from this kind of competition. The result would be that the young son ends up snatching the father's young wife. The father, being fully conscious of this, removes the potential danger before it is too late. Thus, he helps the teenage child build his own home and live there.

These parents may not be mistaken. Maybe they had seen this happen, or they intuitively know what might likely happen. Fifteen years ago, I witnessed an incident with my own eyes. Papa Joe was about sixty years old. He had lost his first wife a few years before. Papa Joe had a friend around his age. This friend decided to give his daughter to him to marry. He sympathized with Papa Joe staying alone. Papa Joe needed someone to prepare his food, thus his friend's daughter was a good choice for him. Everything went well, and Papa Joe got married to this teenage girl. She was fresh and beautiful. Her hairstyle was charming. Every young person also wanted to marry her. Nevertheless, it was already late. Papa Joe in his sixties was the lucky choice, thanks to patriotic friends.

Papa Joe got married as planned. Not long after, still within the honeymoon period, I stood along the road chatting with friends. Suddenly, we saw a young man of about twenty-five ran past us. He was steadfast, consistent in speed and magnificent in style. We watched with amazement and commented that another Timothy Lekunze was born in our hometown. That would be great luck. Just as we were commenting on this, another man, in his sixties, emerged from behind with a tired breath. He was carrying a one and a half meter "cry die" gun. Though he could not speed up as his son, he held the gun in style. In many ways, he would resemble Norman Schwarzkopf commanding the first gulf war. Papa Joe claimed to be that one, who shoots and fires without missing. We thought again that maybe Don Quixote of La Mancha was born in our hometown. If he were born in our hometown, then people suffering from stress and depression would not need a doctor, because they would laugh these ailments away. Unfortunately, all we thought of was not so.

Papa Joe's twenty-five year old son had amused himself with Papa Joe's teenage wife. Papa Joe shouted these words as he dragged behind his son with the "cry die" gun: "That child has taken my wife, I must shoot him down!" Papa Joe was in limbo and his son too. Should Papa Joe shoot down his son to get out of limbo? What can his son do to get out of limbo too? This Papa Joe's son died nine years ago in his early thirties. Papa Joe died last year in his late seventies. What is in this world? Everything is vanity. What are we looking for in this world?

A certain philosopher in the bible, in the book of Ecclesiastes has said it all, that we are catching the wind in this world. He says, "Everything is vanity of vanities. All things and life are full of weariness. I got myself servants. I made myself gardens and orchards. I gather for myself silver and gold…"The list goes on and on; this man has taken that man's wife. This one stole that one's car or money. This man wants to seize my land. He owns a house in America, London, China. His car cost 1 million dollars. There are beds in England and America costing $100 000. Though we say these beds are in America and Europe, if you enter the homes of some rich Africans, you could see them quietly lying in these beds. Nobody knows about this in public. This philosopher writes and tells us about "vanity of vanities." However, this does not mean we should be lazy. After all, if you honestly work and become rich, you are free to spend that money in ways that please you. What we shout at the top of our voices is those people who have embezzled our monies make us suffer, but certainly they are suffering as well in their own ways.

From this story about Papa Joe, we see that these people are not mistaken in having matured males go and live separately in their own homes. For these children will not fail to cause problems if they stay around too long. They must go. We cannot take this as an incidental affair. Parents in the North must have learnt this from some experience in one way or the other. Everything is in limbo; we are in limbo.

Chapter 9
Coping with High Temperatures

Temperatures are very high in the North of Cameroon. When visitors come during the rainy season, between the months of June and October, they claim they feel too hot. However, for the Northerners or people who have been living in the North for long, they feel somehow normal. They already know that the real heat is from the month of February to May, when temperatures reach47 degrees centigrade. Normally, between the months of June and October, temperatures range from 36 to 38 degrees centigrade. Visitors may consider this temperature as very high and not be able to stand the heat. Sometimes, to the surprise of all, there are regular downpours. If I say regular, it means there may be a downpour every week. With the regular downpours, places are cool. Temperatures drop a little, and people feel good. Despite the rains, visitors will still complain of heat because, even after the rains, temperatures cannot drop to the levels in southern Cameroon.

After the rainy season, there is the dry season from October or November. The nights are very cold from November to the end of January, but the days are still very hot. The nights are as cold as in southern Cameroon, and many people get sick because of the cold nights. Many people catch colds and influenza. It seems as if the cold makes people sick in the North, more so than in other parts of the country. During this period, you hardly meet someone who does not have a cold.

After this period of cold nights and hot afternoons, there is another transition. This is the period from March to May or

June depending on when the rains start falling. The highest heat begins in February and will only cease when the rains begin to fall. This period is absolutely the hottest.

If there is luck, the rains begin in May. If no luck, they only begin in June. The months of March, April and May are the hottest. If you want to visit the North, if it is not so urgent, you had better not come in a time that falls in these three months. The heat is unbearable. It is very hot in and outdoors. If you are lucky to be in an area where you have enough water, maybe you soak yourself in water every two or three hours. Just like a duck dries off almost immediately after plunging itself in water, so too you dry up very soon after soaking yourself in water. There is no need for a towel during this period. Immediately you soak yourself in water, you feel very cool as if there is no heat. You feel good. However, just wait for ten or fifteen minutes. You start feeling some kind of beautiful warmth, and you are happy. Just when you start feeling that warmness, give yourself another five minutes; the heat is already there again. For many others and me, at bedtime, we use a trick as we go to bed. At bedtime, when I am in the city, I open the shower tap and water pours on me. Then without drying myself, I rush to bed immediately. I fall asleep at once so that before my body dries up, I am deep in sleep, then I do not feel the heat. When I am in Carrefour Poli where I do not have enough water, I sprinkle myself with a bit of water and rush to bed. God gave me a gift. I hear some people say they cannot sleep. When I lie on the bed, I give myself only a few seconds to be asleep. Nevertheless, without soaking or rubbing myself with water, my mind cannot settle to sleep. After three or four hours of sleep, I am up to rub, sprinkle or bath myself in water again.

During this time, you will drink a lot of water. Many times, you have drunk water until your stomach is as round as a calabash and paining. Despite the paining calabash stomach, you are still thirsty and continue to drink more water. The stomach is finally as round as that of a spider. I measured the amount of water for two consecutive days that I drank in Carrefour Poli. I saw I was drinking six litres a day. Drinking this amount of water in Carrefour Poli where we lack water is already too much. Drinking six litres a day, how about the water to cook food, how about water with which to take shower? Those "big people" who drink only bottled water, if they have to drink six litres a day, it costs them 3000 francs ($6) per day for drinking water alone. That is not easy. I also measured the amount of urine I passed out in a day, and I was not sure it was up to two litres. It is clear that when you drink water, by sweating and respiration, all the water is gone and you have to drink more.

For those in cities where there is electricity, some people are able to procure fans. Not everyone is able to use fans regularly because their use inflates electricity bills. The majority of the people are not able to pay electricity bills of up to 5000 francs ($10) a month. Therefore, many people may have fans but still be unable to use them regularly. They may use the fans periodically, during the days that the heat is unbearable. Nevertheless, at times, when the heat gets too strong, the fans are no longer helpful. The fans turn and blow the air onto you all right, but instead of cold or cool wind falling on you, the air or wind is instead very hot. It is not fresh air. At this level, you do not have an option but to turn off the fan and maybe run out of the house or room.

Air conditioners are only available in some government offices, banks, enterprises and companies. I would say less than two percent of the population is able to afford an air conditioner at home. The top businesspersons can afford them in their homes. Only government officials at the top would be able to afford air conditioning at home. Even the priest cannot afford it. Having an air conditioner itself is not the problem. The problem is to pay the bills. You may pay the electricity bills but have no food on the table, how sad. If you cannot afford a fan or an air conditioner, then what do you do? Maybe you pray to god. Maybe you go and join yourself to what opposes heat, which is water. Drink water, bath in it as many times as possible. Unfortunately, water is not so common.

Almost everyone sleeps outside on their mats during these hottest months. But I lack the heart to sleep outside. I fear snakes, scorpions and centipedes. The heat causes all the snakes to come out of their holes. They are everywhere. They want to seize the village from us. I have a terrible fear of snakes. I cannot stand the thought of a snake on or by me as I lie on that mat outside. Despite the snakes everywhere, Northerners are used to sleeping outside without any fear. Going around the villages, you see many snakes and people already bitten by snakes, but people do not care. They continue to sleep outside. At night, they go around without torches, as I mentioned before.

Nevertheless, I think that some of them fear snakes as they go around, but when the snake is gone, that fear disappears. I say this because one evening, around 7:30 pm, my neighbour's wife shouted, "Teacher, teacher, I have seen a snake." She held a near death torch in her hands, with which she could not see well. I came with my "bright star" torch and searched everywhere and could not find the snake. As we stood there, I saw how she was afraid. I observed how her legs were trembling because of fear. She showed me a hole near her kitchen that the snake must have got into. Despite all her fear, I saw how she, her husband and their two children still slept outside on the mat that same night. For "out of sight is out of mind." As soon as the snake was out of sight, fear disappeared and she had a sound sleep.

We spend a lot of time sitting under trees. Trees provide good shade during the day. It is very cool under these trees, and we wish our rooms could be as cool. It is unfortunate that people are felling trees without pity. They know the importance of these trees, but they do not allow them to stand. Their rooms are small and tiny. They cannot sit inside when there is the heat, and the only cool place is under trees outside. You see a tree today, and in the next few weeks, that tree may be gone. If they keep cutting the trees at this rate without replanting, in some years to come, it will be excruciatingly difficult.

Not only do people have problems with the heat. Animals do as well. In places where there is a bit of water, people and animals are all there. Snakes, lizards, frogs, scorpions, and centipedes are all there. Sheep and goats are there. The heat forces all animals to go out and find the least bit of water or cool place. So if water drips on your floor or around your house, be careful because unwelcome guests may come and stay. When you extend your arm into a cool place in your room, or a wet cloth, be careful, a snake may already be lying there.

Overall, everyone does what he or she can to cope with the intense heat. As the days pass by, that long awaited first downpour may come in May or June for that year. After this first downpour, there are hopes that more will come and that the temperatures will drop. Everything is in limbo. We are in limbo.

Chapter 10
Ritualistic Circumcision

I told you in a previous chapter we would talk about circumcision. Thanks be to god, we have finally arrived. He has kept us alive so far, owe can write and read more again. Muslims and some tribes' people in the North do not circumcise their male children immediately after birth. They circumcise these children at a later date, when the children are between the ages of five and ten. Circumcision in itself, even done at the age of fifteen, is not a ritual. What makes it a ritual is the way people do it. What happens before, during and after circumcision is what makes it a ritual.

Circumcision is done in the forest, and the children have to live there for about a month. For this reason, they must attain that age where they can live in the forest. The villagers told me that, some years ago, these children had to live in this jungle for at least three months. The government had to step in. The government made the parents understood that making children stay away for three months was not healthy for the education of the child. This is the truth. If a child stays out of school for three months, even if the child is very intelligent, I think it would be unfair to promote that child to the next class. If a child stays out of school for three months, this can be the beginning of the end of the child's formal education. With this advice from the government, villagers reduced the period of stay in the jungle to a month.

Before children go to the forest for circumcision, parents organize traditional festivities. They pray and ask for blessings and protection from god and the ancestors. This is necessary. For the children to live in the forest for a month is like a war.

73

The parents do not take this lightly, because we do not know if these children will return alive. The maternal uncles of the child or children bring a goat for the ceremony. The father spends much money too in preparation of food and drinks. Children of the poor may wait up to the age of fifteen, because their families lack the money to procure the things necessary for such a ceremony.

After the ceremony at home, the children go into the jungle where the circumcision is done. May be done by one of the village person who is an expert in those matters. They live in the forest for a month. Food is prepared, and a woman of menopause takes the food to them every day. This food is "fufu cornmeal" (of course).

The boys have a male guide who is an expert in the traditions and dances of the people. Every day, this hero teaches the children how to sing and dance. They play the drums, dance every evening, and sleep on mats they carried along with them. They also shower every day at 5 pm. It is very sacred in the jungle. The guide sees to it that no other person visits the children.

You are not informed if your child dies in the forest. He will be buried without your knowledge. The "fufu corn" that you send to your child everyday will be sunned and made to dry. The other boys and their guide store the food in a bag every day. They hand the sack of food to the child's mother the day they return from the forest. That is when you will understand that your child died in the forest.

The day of victory finally comes when the one month is over, and the children have to go home. On this day of victory, the children accompanied by their guide will return home very early in the morning before sunrise. Each parent (father) takes his child/children to his own house. They are locked and fed inside the house, and nobody sees them. At 9 pm on the same day, they come out of the room, putting on their new clothes and shoes. They cover their entire head with loincloth. Since their return in the morning, their mothers have not seen them. Their mothers see them only when they come out of the room at 9 pm. However, how can their mothers see their hidden faces under the loincloths? They have to chip in a few coins (money), placing them in the children's palms, so the children will open their faces for their mothers to see.

They are free now. They can visit their friends. They visit only friends and boys who have passed through the same ceremony before them. Any boy who has not yet passed through this ceremony is not an equal, he is below them, and thus they cannot visit him. They also pay a visit to the Hardo (chief) as men, and the "Hardo" welcomes them and sees them as men. The "Hardo" or "Lamido" is very happy to see them. He is fully aware that new men are born in the village on that very day. Thus, his village is growing, as there are good signs for continuity.

In the villages, it is obligatory for the members of certain tribes and ethnic groups to go through this ceremony. Nevertheless, if they live in towns and cities, parents may see this as a dangerous and unthinkable undertaking. This is because their children do not live in the village. Parents of these city children cannot imagine how they can suddenly carry their children to live in these dark forests or jungles for one month. These children would certainly be frightened. Whatever the name is, whether circumcision or ritual, it will not work for them.

In any case, he who survives the one-month jungle life is different among his peers. Surviving in the midst of poisonous snakes and predatory animals is already a sign that they are different. Those who have never been there cannot speak about it, because experience is the best teacher. The children who have been there and survived have reason to be proud.

Chapter 11
Surviving in the Midst of Snakes

I told you in one of the previous chapters that something kicked me out of my hard-earned room. We have to talk about that unfortunate incident in this chapter.

After surviving without electricity and water in the scorching heat, there is still one more element. This element is the snake. If you survive the snakes, it is possible that you have overcome it all. If you survive the snakes, were there a snake nation, maybe you would be the president of that nation and if not, you would occupy an important position. Snakes are everywhere during the day and night. Day and night in limbo. Everything is in limbo, limbo everywhere. When you sit, you see the snakes coming. When you sit, you see them going. When you sit, you see them falling. When you sit, you see them climbing trees. In short, when you sit, you see them coming, going, falling and climbing. Some are fat, some are thin, some are long, and some are small like a lock of hair on your head. Nobody told me, but I saw two snakes already almost as tiny as a lock of the hair on my head. Nevertheless, be very careful! A small snake may be very dangerous. A snake may be tiny, but its poison may not be small. They have all kinds of colours; black, green, brownish red, dull white with black marks. The North is a land of snakes. I do not think snakes area protected species in Cameroon. In other words, if snakes are not a protected species in Cameroon, those people who trap snakes and sell them around the world should come to the North of Cameroon and get them.

One day, I was in Garoua for the weekend. I got up around 2 am and opened the toilet door, and a snake was inside. Because the house is well built, without openings for snakes to come in through, I wondered how the snake got in. Probably it got in through the small toilet catchment that stayed open behind the house. Once it got into the catchment, it then entered one of the pipes and climbed into the toilet room. In this same house, before going to bed every night, I always flash a touch under the bed. One night, I sat in my "asana" posture and did my regular meditations for about an hour. I lay on the bed, flashed my torch under the bed and saw a snake right there. This snake might have come in through the main door or still, through the toilet. It could have then come into my room, because I always keep my bedroom door open. I realized I had just meditated for an hour with a snake under the bed. What if it had climbed on me?

If you live on the outskirts of the city where there is grass around, always keep the doors of your house closed, otherwise snakes will make themselves at home in your house. I mean if you are rich enough to build a good house without openings. For a normal villager, it is not easy for them to have such a house. In Garoua, where I go for weekends and holidays, our house is outside of the city centre. I cannot count the number of times I have met with snakes around the house. These encounters take place in the yard, as we always keep the doors closed.

However, there is one door, which is always open because it is the bar. One weekend when I returned from Carrefour Poli, I heard about a snake incident that happened in the bar. The lights had ceased. It was already 7 pm. The man selling in the bar was standing outside. Suddenly, he saw a giant black snake getting into the bar. He ran and followed it, but it was too late. The snake was right there inside the bar. The barman called for the two customers who were sitting outside drinking to come and help him kill the snake. They came and saw the snake but went back to their seats and continued drinking. They told him that the snake was too big and that it was dangerous trying to kill it. They told him to try to chase the snake away. He called for many people around, but all of them refused to attempt to kill the snake. The snake was inside the bar until 9 pm, when he found someone who accepted to help him kill that snake. The man tried and only killed it around 10 pm. They told me that this snake was barking like a dog each time they touched it.

We may now turn our attention to the snake stories of Carrefour Poli. There are snakes everywhere around my room, which I built in Carrefour Poli. I see snakes during the day and at night. One day in the dark, I was sitting on my bed. I flashed the torch and saw a snake penetrating through a very tiny hole between the doorframe and the wall. I had thought that all openings were completely blocked, but I was mistaken. If you are in a snake environment, never think you have blocked all the openings. This opening was so small that I never spotted it. However, snakes know all openings. Even at night, when I go out to pee, flashing the torch, I see a snake lying somewhere. There are evenings I see two or three snakes around my house.

Taking vows is not a good thing, except when you are very sure of what you are doing. I vowed many times and failed to respect my promise. One day, I had killed snakes until I was tired of them. I thought it was already too much. Therefore, I vowed that I would no longer kill snakes. I vowed, from that day henceforth, that when I see a snake, I would let it go. After this vow, I travelled for the weekend to Garoua. Just as I entered the house, my little niece called, "Uncle, uncle, a snake." I rushed, get a stick and killed that little viper. I regretted my vow of the previous day. Yet, I forgave myself. If masters like Peter failed in their vows, then what more of a poor soul like me? I hate killing things in general. If I see a rat in the house, I just want to chase it away. Bats come into the house, and I just chase them away too. Man and snake do not go together. There is deep hatred between the two. When I see a snake, even if it goes away, I always feel that my number one enemy has escaped. Enemies can reconcile and forgive one another, but I doubt if man and snake will reconcile.

Despite the fact that these snakes were all around my house, I had no fear. I built my room. I wanted to live in it. Teachers earn little salaries, and I knew that the little money I could save from rents was important. More so, health was the most important. I built my room with much ventilation and freshness that should enhance my health. Despite all this mathematical and logical thinking about why I must not abandon my room for snakes, something happened at last. This night was the most worrisome night in my life. Everything was in limbo.

During this evening, I sat as usual listening to BBC (British Broadcasting Corporation) on my radio. After sitting for a while, I felt uneasy. I had a feeling I should walk up to the Carrefour or crossroads where everyone meets to speak true stories, events or lies. It is good to sit under that big neem tree. The men who are a little informed want to speak football all the time. They say every year Eto'o Fils is the best player in the world. I say no, Eto'o Fils was never voted the world's best player. I say, it is Lionel Messi. Trouble will begin. They will ask, "If he is not the best player in the world, why is he the best paid player in the world?" They say, Eto'o Fils scored more goals than Lionel Messi. I say no, and tell them the number of goals Messi has scored. They are completely unaware that Messi still scores many goals since Eto'o Fils left Barcelona. Eto'o may be the best paid player but not necessarily the richest. Dare say there is another player in the world richer than he and see bulldogs barking at you. Well, it is just the facts I tell them.

Eto'o Fils is a master. If every human being could master his profession as Eto'o Fils has mastered his, the world would be a far better place. If the politicians and economists could work politics and economics like Eto'o Fils has mastered football, they would become statesmen and women and corruption and poverty would vanish at the blink of an eye. If every medical doctor could master his job as Eto'o Fils has done football, most lives would be safe. If engineers could master road construction as Eto'o has mastered football, the potholes on our roads would be far fewer. We should honour masters like Eto'o Fils who have given all in their professions.

Well, on my way to our Carrefour where we meet and talk or just sit and observe, I changed my mind and instead returned home. I do not know where that thought came from, but it said, "Tardif, go back home." It was around 6:30 pm. I turned and headed home again. Arriving home, I pulled a chair from the house to sit outside. However, a thought came to me again, that mosquitoes had bit me outside last evening. Therefore, I pulled my chair back into the house and sat inside. All along, my small portable radio was in my hands. I continued listening to BBC –Focus on Africa. All the while, my torch too was in my hands. I am always fully aware of the danger of snakes, so my torch is always in my hands in the darkness. It is almost impossible for me to step on a snake. I watch everywhere I step most carefully. I believe nobody is more careful than I concerning where he puts his feet.

It was already almost 7 pm, and I was sitting on this chair still listening to "Focus on Africa." I held the radio in my left hand, close to my left ear. I held my torch in my right hand. In the dark room, I knew I could need the torch in an emergency at any time. I leaned backward on my chair. Oh BBC, how nice…! In the dark village, in my dark room, far away from the world, BBC brings me the world. I knew everything happening. Even if I lived in that dark village for a year without going out, I would still be conscious of everything going on. My small portable radio cost me just 2500 francs ($5), and I spend about a dollar every month for its batteries. How cheap this is; it successfully fuels me with all the latest news around the world. I feel connected, I am not lost, and I feel one with the world, with the universe, thanks to BBC.

BBC news was different this night. Impossible things were happening. Gaddafi had fallen, Barack Obama had caught Osama Bin Laden, Lionel Messi almost scored seven goals. I was absorbed in the news. Wonders shall never end. Wow, BBC! The news took me far and deep. As when Napoleon Bonaparte became the revolution itself, as when the master meditated until he became the meditation itself, I too was absorbed into the news until I became the news itself. I had forgotten all the darkness. I was not even aware of where I was. It was a very nice world. A peaceful state of mind where there are no snakes. Yet at this state of total tranquillity, I was not dumb dead. My conscious mind was still aware of the least movements that could take place on or around me. Just as I was listening and almost repeating to myself that only unimaginable things were happening, my own unimaginable was right there just a few seconds away.

I suddenly felt something on my left lap close to my knee. I had a feeling it was either a scorpion or a centipede. Still holding my radio to my left ear, I raised my right hand, switched on the torch, and pointed it to my lap. What did I see? Hey, BBC! A viper, about 20 centimetres long comfortably wrapped itself on my left lap with its head a little raised. Everything is in limbo. I was in limbo. What could I do? With my hands raised, my two legs raised, my eyes widely opened, my mouth opened 360 degrees, I shouted as I fell backward. To my surprise, I found myself standing on my bed, which was about 150 centimetres from me, behind me. Maybe a certain Angel carried me to that bed. I did not know how or when I reached this bed. It is actually true that when man is in serious trouble, he can fly. I do not know what blocked my voice. I intended to shout at the top of my voice, but instead it came out like the voice of a little baby. Maybe the fear paralyzed my voice. To my surprise too, my torch did not leave my hands. The fact that I held the torch tight in my right hand was a mystery to me. I was totally out of control physically and mentally. In short, in that very moment, I acted mechanically because I was not thinking. I was not able to control my thoughts and movements. I only came to my senses when I realized myself on that bed. For a split of a second, I was out of my mind.

One day my students saw a small pole near my bed and asked me what it was doing there. I told them it was for snakes. I flashed the torch. I stretched my hand and got the pole. I pointed the torch on the floor. The snake was lying there with its head raised in my direction ready to strike. I pointed the pole and stood watching the snake as if to kill it, or not. For quite some time, I stood there watching the snake. I felt my body heavy as a rock. I felt as if my legs developed taproots that went far and deep into the depth of the earth. With its head raised in my direction, the snake too stayed fixed to its spot. The snake did not make even the slightest movement. I gazed at the snake, fixed, with no movements. The snake too gazed at me, fixed, with no movements. If snakes could fly, maybe that snake might have flown to me.

Suddenly my torch was dying down. If the torch completely died down, it meant I would have to face the snake in complete darkness. How would that work? Therefore, I hurried and pounded the snake with the stick. After killing the snake, I tried to look at my legs and arms to see if anything bad had happened. I saw fresh blood oozing out of my right arm. I was confused and did not know if the snake had bitten me as it lay on my lap. I called my neighbour. He looked for a motorbike and accompanied me to the health centre that night. I asked the nurse to do the test, because there was a possibility I might have been wounded in the course of the struggle. He said there was nothing he could use to test to see whether it was a snake bite except a "black stone." Unfortunately, he said he was not in possession of a "black stone" at that very moment. I carried the snake with me, and he said since it was a viper, it was better to administer anti-venom at once rather than waiting for the test. After the injection, I asked that they show me my bed. The nurse asked me, "Which bed?" I said the bed I would sleep on. He told me I had to go back to my home and only return in the morning for the next injection. I asked if he expected me to go and sleep in that same room again. The nurse encouraged me to return home, which I did.

When I reached my room, with the fear that another snake may fall, I went straight into bed inside the mosquito net. If the next snake were to fall, at least it would not reach me because it would slide on the net and fall, or it might hang on. Nevertheless, I had dreams of struggling with snakes all night long. In some of the dreams, I was flying in the air, and the snakes were flying after me. In some, the snakes surrounded me. In some, I saw snakes hunting for me same as a dog hunts for mole rats. I am sure I slept less than three hours that night. In the morning, I found my radio lying scattered. I packed it and replaced the antenna that was broken. After two years as I write this story, the radio still stands by me. I am still listening to BBC. What is the news today on BBC? The world's catholic community has a new Pope. How strange that Pope Benedict xvi resigns; this is uncommon in the church's tradition. The new Pope has taken the name of Pope Francis 1. More news: Barcelona FC comes from two goals down to beat AC Milan in the champions league four goals to zero, qualifying for the quarter finals. Lionel Messi again, scoring twice. BBC, wonders shall never end.

I went to the health centre, and the second injection was administered. From there, I continued home to Garoua where I stayed for the next one week. I administered the rest of the injections myself. There is a saying from The Kybalion which states that "As above, so below; as below, so above." I watched the snakes every day below me. At last, the snakes came from above to fall on me. A man told me a short story when I arrived in the North four years ago. I was asking him how they go about every night, wearing slippers and without torches when snakes are everywhere. He said nothing happens to them. He said there is a story about a certain man most careful of snakes. One day while riding his horse, a snake fell on him from a tree and bit him. I reflected on this after I suffered from this incident. This story was a message to me, something that would happen to me four years later. If I were a wise man, I should have understood this. We must honour men and women who have wisdom, because they will rescue us in times of need and free us from unnecessary suffering and hardship. Man is not safe in this world. When the time comes for the unfortunate to happen, it does happen. Even if you are most careful, you will still face it. Therefore, prayer is necessary. Everything is limbo. Man is in limbo.

By the time I was building this room, I made it large enough, with large windows and good ventilation. This would reduce the heat. I had thatched it with grass, because it would not be as hot as a roof of corrugated sheets. Never did I know that snakes would climb into the thatched grass roof and fall on me. I had intuitively felt this coming though. Sometimes I looked at the roof and feared snakes falling from there. The reason for wrapping my bed with a mosquito net was not really against mosquitoes. I feared snakes falling on me when I would sleep. So when you fear something, know it is your intuition warning you. Think hard about it and take the necessary actions to prevent the danger from happening. We suffer a lot in Africa because we lack foresight. A bridge will collapse and kill people before we rush to repair or renew it. A bank will collapse with peoples' savings before we know something was wrong. Cholera will sweep away entire populations before we know people are not drinking good water. Fire will burn down whole properties before we know that firefighters should be well positioned in strategic points with better equipment. Bank robberies have taken place not just once in plain daylight in this country, yet there are no measures to stop them. The list can go on forever, for there is a saying that there is a beginning and no end for evil. Everything is limbo. We are in limbo.

This snake incident caused me to abandon this room. On my return to Carrefour Poli, I had to look for a new room. It took me two days to get a new room. I still had to sleep in my room for those two days. In these two days, I never sat on a chair inside the room. It was dangerous to sit, for a falling snake may just lie on you. I stood up all the time in the room with my big hat. A falling snake would slide on the hat straight to the floor. When cooking, I stood with the pot on the stove. After all, if another snake should fall in the pot with hot oil inside, I would not need my stick, for the hot oil would do it all. Then at night, I stayed out at the Carrefour, and at 8 or 9 pm I returned and went straight to bed inside the net. When I was abandoning the room, the people of the village laughed at me. I told them that I would never live in a house thatched with grass again. Prevention is better than cure, as the saying goes. Although snakes have many tricks, it is still better to avoid their ways.

I heard a few months later that my maternal step aunt returned from the farm one evening, very tired. It was getting dark. It was in the village, and there was no electricity. She got into the house and saw a black plastic bag lying on the floor. She stretched her hand out to pick it up. Just as she was about to pick up the plastic bag, she was bitten by a snake. Yes, the black plastic bag was a black snake. You have to be careful, because snakes have all kinds of tricks. They overpower mans' intelligence. Maybe to successfully fight snakes, we need wisdom instead of knowledge.

In these grass roofs, scorpions, centipedes and snakes are the unwelcomed guests. This snake incident occurred when I returned from the summer holiday, after my room had stayed locked for about three months. The people of Carrefour Poli told me that snakes came in because the house had stayed uninhabited for too long. They told me that after staying out for so long like that, I should have made a big fire in the house. The intense heat and smoke would drive all the snakes away. Some told me that I should have sprayed the room with strong-smelling insecticide and locked the door for three days, then all evil and snakes would have left the house. Some told me to tie a large mat above my bed, so that when snakes are falling, they hang on it. After hanging on the mat, however, would the snake fly away? They would still fall to the floor, eventually.

The shock of this snake incident was so heavy on me. I was actually in limbo. It was difficult for me to handle. I thanked people for all the unproven, unpractical and unscientific methods of keeping snakes away from a thatched house. I was still sceptical; a house where snakes fall from the roof is not the house in which I wanted to live. I wanted no part of that thatched roof. I left the room and got a two-room house, roofed with corrugated sheets.

I think that anybody who has lived or who is living in the North of Cameroon, not in the city centre, must have a funny snake story to tell. If we collect all these stories in a book, I am sure it will make a very big book. I have just told mind. If you have one, I am ready to listen.

Chapter 12
The Millennium Development Goals and their Attainment in Carrefour Poli, other villages in Cameroon and Africa as a Whole

The Millennium Development Goals (MDGs) are development goals set by the United Nations. Each of the goals has specific targets and dates for achieving those targets. Goals set in 2000 were to be achieved by the year 2015. The aim of the MDGs is to encourage development and improve social and economic conditions in the world's poorest countries. All heads of state adopted the United Nations Millennium Declaration.

Since world leaders adopted this millennium declaration, the whole world and humanity as a whole were awakened and very happy about it. Musicians started singing it, writers started writing it, teachers started teaching it and sculptors started carving it. The greatest, richest and most powerful nations on earth, represented by their great finance ministers, filled the big banks with money. Their intention was to see that these goals were attained. Enough funds were poured into the World Bank, the International Monetary Fund (IMF) and the African Development Bank. The debts of the Heavily Indebted Poor Countries (HIPC) were cancelled. The aim of this action was to allow impoverished countries to re-channel the resources saved from the forgiven debts to social programs for improving health and education and for alleviating poverty.

Cameroon fell among the heavily indebted poor countries and therefore benefitted from this program. The debts of the nation of Cameroon were forgiven, thus she had to channel the debt payment funds to development projects in health and education.

Let us say Carrefour Poli is the microcosm of Cameroon and Africa as a whole. Most African countries also benefitted from this program. If this program has been successful in Carrefour Poli, the microcosm, it might mean the macrocosm (Cameroon and Africa) as a whole also benefitted. The MDGs are eight in number, and a certain region may make progress toward some goals more than others. In general, how the goals have worked in Carrefour Poli may be a reflection of what we have elsewhere in Cameroon and Africa as a whole.

Let's look at the goals and see what has been happening since their birth in the year 2000.

Goal: Eradicate Extreme Poverty and Hunger. When you live in Carrefour Poli, you may conclude that this goal has not been attained. More than half of the population is probably living on less than a dollar a day. Children drop out of school because their parents cannot afford 2000 francs ($4) a year to pay for their tuition. People move in the dry season because they cannot afford the monthly water maintenance cost of500 francs ($1). Go around the village, live with the people as I have lived with them for the past five years. You will not refute what I am saying. The people are poor, and if Carrefour Poli is a microcosm of the macrocosm, urgent action needs to be taken as far as this goal is concerned.

Positive action is possible if the goal planners and executers focus on the activities that people work on daily to earn money. What could that be but agriculture? Although the farming season is short, the people of Carrefour Poli are still farmers. If the cost of farm inputs is reduced, it would mean that people could cultivate more than they do presently and thus have more money. Most of the people cannot cultivate corn because they cannot afford inorganic fertilizers. A bag of fertilizer costs about 24 000 francs ($48) here in the North. This amount of money is already too much for an average farmer. To cultivate an acre of corn farm, the farmer would need five bags of this fertilizer. This is something almost impossible for the people of Carrefour Poli. The musicians have sung about the reduction of poverty, but if we have not gone to the fields to apply it, it means we have failed. Money and hunger go together. If people are poor, it means they are hungry too. I tis not just about having a meal. What is the quality of the meal? Filling the stomach, every day, year after year, with lumps of "fufu corn" without meat, fish and vegetables will weaken man, woman and child. In the end, the body cannot resist disease. Everything is now a chain. Poverty-hunger-disease-suffering and death. More than half of the population cannot afford one decent meal in a week. There is lack of vigour because of no nutritious food, no fruits, no vegetables. People just exist. They do not live. If everywhere in Cameroon and Africa was like this, then this goal has failed, and we need to go back to the drawing boards

Goal: Achieve Universal Primary Education. This goal has been attained to an extent, but the target for this goal is too high. The United Nations may try to revise the target. The target states that by 2015, all children complete a full course of primary schooling, both girls and boys. It may be a curse setting five years targets; meanwhile it may take fifty years to attain universal primary education.

In Carrefour Poli, even in class three children leave school for marriage. Many too did not even enrol in school.

There are good progress indicators for this goal: school enrolment is higher, the state has created many schools, pupils do not walk long distances to school. Some might not have gone to school in the past, because schools were far away from many homes. Though enrolment is higher, the target set is too high. The boys drop out of school same as the girls. If I am to rank the goals in chronological order according to how they shall be attained in the North as a whole, maybe I would rank this one as the last to be attained. If all of Cameroon and Africa is like Carrefour Poli, I would say it will certainly take time before this goal is attained the way the United Nations states it. Good progress is made as far as this goal is concerned, but this does not mean it will soon be attained. It will take so many more years in the North before seeing more than 90% of children successfully complete primary education. School enrolment is one thing, and the quality of education is one thing too. A lot of teachers are recruited, but many schools still do not have the required number of teachers. Although there are parent-employed teachers, nothing is certain about the quality of their output, and they may not always be available either.

Goal: Promote Gender Equality and Empower Women. As far as this goal is concerned in Carrefour Poli, more girls go to school, and gender disparity does not exist in school. I think most of the parents are fully conscious that their girls as well as their boys need to go to school. Nevertheless, deep-rooted cultural habits may hinder this goal from its complete realization. People let girls do house chores, cook food, and fetch firewood and water. Meanwhile, boys might sit or be busy learning how to ride a motorbike. This has to change, but it will take time to change, because these habits are deeply rooted in culture, religion and general beliefs. If in other parts of Cameroon and Africa parents still view the girl child as the doer of all house work and the fetcher of water and wood, then it is a big hindrance to seeing this goal fully realized.

Empowering women and the girl child is attained, but changing things that are deeply rooted in cultures is a big task. And although parents want their girl children to study, you still see cases where these children are withdrawn from school and handed over for marriage. If a girl child successfully completes primary school, the parents start thinking of getting her married to a man. Some do go to secondary school, but few finally graduate. However, there is hope for the girl child more than ever before.

Goal: Reduce Child Mortality: Under this goal, we have targets like reducing mortality among children under the age of five, which includes the need to vaccinate infants against measles and other diseases. To an extent, I think this goal is successful in Carrefour Poli. Every year health workers come around for vaccination. There is a major campaign for de-worming primary school children. Health workers come around to schools and share Praziquantel and Mebendazole with all the children. These drugs should be helping these children a lot, by ridding them of intestinal parasites and worms, especially tapeworms that could cause many a problem if it were not for the Praziquantel. A person infested by intestinal worms and parasites will soon have scores of other diseases. Because they do not go to the hospital, these diseases aggravate their health and can even lead to death. Health officials come to schools and chief palaces and administer yellow fever and meningitis vaccines. Also, a lot is going on for the administration of the polio vaccine to all children from zero to five years. This has helped us in

Carrefour Poli, and if it is similar everywhere in Cameroon and Africa, we are on the road to meeting this goal.

There is general awareness among people about attending to the health of children. Mothers take it seriously whenever there is a vaccination team around. They do all things possible to get their children there. Although most people lack the spirit of going to the hospital, this does not mean that some do not go. Many do take their children to the hospital or health centres when they are sick. Overall, there is general awareness of health, even if I wish parents were more careful about the water they give to their children to drink. Child mortality must have fallen somehow in Carrefour Poli. I hope it has done so in the rest of Cameroon and Africa as a whole.

Goal: Improve Maternal Health. In Carrefour Poli there is awareness of mothers' health to an extent. Some of the pregnant women go regularly to the clinic. Most of them deliver at home. The fact that, during difficult deliveries, they might find ways to rush the woman to the health centre or hospital is a good sign. The government has opened health centres in villages. Health personnel are employed to attend to pregnant women. Even if medically trained personnel do not attend all births, midwives are around, and some village women have been educated and trained by these health personnel to handle deliveries at home. There are still some headstrong couples that even the hardest metal will not crack. I am referring to the couple that still believes the wife should give birth alone, while her husband stands behind the house with his raised rabbit ears and rushes into the house when he hears the baby's cry.

Maternal health to an extent has improved in Carrefour Poli. I have met men who told me their wives are taking the injectable contraceptives every three months to prevent unwanted pregnancies. They know that birth control is important for the family. I have met some men who have preferred to be monogamous. They do not only want to stay with one wife, but they express the wish to have only about four children. They start to feel that it is not only about having children. It is a matter of eating well and educating the children. They have learnt about family planning. If Cameroon and Africa as a whole continue like this, in some years to come, much will have been attained. Despite this, there is still much we can do. There are dotted successes here and there in the crowd. Nevertheless, they are still good signs, for not everybody walks the same speed.

Goal: Combat HIV/AIDS, Malaria and Other Diseases. A lot has been achieved under this goal. Take sensitization about HIV/AIDS. The government and non-governmental organizations have done a lot of work in this area. People have been sensitized and re-sensitized, and we have become conscious of the reality of HIV/AIDS. Even children know about this canker worm that ravaged across Africa like wildfire. This might be the most attainable of the millennium goals. Those needing the HIV antiretroviral drugs may receive them for free. Before these antiretroviral drugs came, African people were dying in their numbers. Today, HIV positive people take these drugs, look healthy and fresh, and live longer. Before the arrival of these drugs, it was a pity to witness the fall of family and friends. People did not only die, but they suffered before dying. They suffered all kinds of infections and diseases. This way of dying was terrible for humankind. Happy is he who does not have to suffer so much from disease before dying.

For malaria, there is affordable and cheap treatment at the hospitals. There are ones that cost only a few dollars for one course of treatment. At home, I always have drugs equivalent to a treatment of one course of uncomplicated malaria. It is good to specify "uncomplicated malaria" because if the malaria is already complicated you need a doctor for sure. When you insist on treating complicated malaria by yourself, you may end up going six feet deep into the earth. Some years ago, this treatment was never there. There was never any simple affordable home treatment for malaria. Nevertheless, it is advisable, if you take the home treatment and do not get better, that you go to the hospital. The government has sensitized citizens very much on how to prevent malaria and how to deal with it if attacked by it. The government has distributed mosquito nets to all homes in Carrefour Poli, and I am sure they are distributed in the whole of Cameroon and maybe throughout Africa. The United Nations, governments and individuals have declared a war against the mosquito. The mosquito is the number one enemy of the African man. If the mosquito was as fat as a cow, I am sure a full-scale war would be declared against it. Coalitions would be formed among nations; ground, sea and air artillery would be employed to fight this common enemy, the mosquito.

Many years ago, in a year full of mosquitos, there were many stories. One of them was about a certain witch woman who asked for riches from Satan. This woman knew fully well that Satan is very cruel, a deceiver of humans and very wicked. Did she expect any good from Satan? In her encounter with him, Satan piled many bags in front of her and asked her to take one. According to Satan, the bag this woman would carry was a big bag of money that would make her rich. Satan told her that she should untie the bag when she arrives home. At home, she was curious and anxious. Her heart was beating rapidly, and her blood pressure must have been very high. She was excited by her riches. She untied the bag and instead of money, mosquitoes came out. These mosquitoes spread everywhere and bit everyone. We had many malaria attacks that year, and many people died. More than fifty mosquitoes could settle on a person at any one time. In a year that this witch fails to ask for riches from Satan, there would be fewer mosquitoes. However, this witch, never caring about the suffering of the population, would still think of her ambition to get rich. The coming year or after a few years, she would again visit Satan, and mosquitoes would be plenty everywhere followed by malaria. Unfortunately, we never caught this witch woman. Maybe she died at last, because there are always mosquitoes, but they have never suddenly appeared in great numbers again maybe for the past seventeen years. There were many stories of these witches coming with different kinds of problems, and we were always told that they were women. We never knew the origin of witches, but we knew they existed. We were always seized with panic when it was announced that the witches were at work. There were the stories about the "cut head" too. These "cut head" witch people went around cutting heads and selling them in Nigeria or to the Whiteman. Our parents instructed that we must walk in groups to avert them.

In the days of the witch people, Africa was still far behind in the news media and the spreading of the news around the world. Today the world is a global village. Almost everyone has at least a radio if not a TV set. The mind is broader, and everyone wants to talk about things happening around the world. Wars around the world, terrorism around the world. People's minds are broader, and they see politics, economics, sports and many things in a wider spectrum. Even if there are the witch people, they are seen differently today than was the case many years ago. And it is like Pandora's Box; we know society cannot attribute all problems to women and treat them as scapegoats.

As a whole, there is general progress in Carrefour Poli, Cameroon and Africa. Children are well taken care of concerning the prevention and treatment of malaria. Other chronic diseases like tuberculosis and typhoid are still present but less rampant. One thing is certain, there is progress and there is hope.

Goal: Ensure Environmental Sustainability. This goal is a challenge in Carrefour Poli. The trees are going. Wood carvers fell trees all the time. The wood carvers are the external parasites infesting the forest. If trees could speak, I am sure they would curse the wood carvers when they approach with their axes and machetes. If the theory of re-incarnation is true, I am sure these wood carvers would return in the next life as agro-forestry technicians to plant and protect trees. In so doing, they would pay back what they destroyed. The villagers do not plant trees; rather they cut trees and use them as firewood. If trees are cut in other parts of Cameroon and Africa like this, I am sure the desert is intensifying. Even the government is felling trees to sell timber in Europe. The fear is that maybe enough replanting is not taking place. We hope, however, that the government is replanting these trees.

Protected species of fish in the North are being caught. The controllers of protected fish species stand on the roadside and take bribes of less than a dollar. This is unfortunate.

Year in and year out, water volumes reduce. All the water in Lake Chad is gone. One day the water track of Lake Chad will be dry. The empty space will then resemble a dead valley.

The threat of species extinction continues and increases. Poachers kill elephants every day. Poachers killed more than one hundred elephants in Waza Park in the North of Cameroon in 2012. They came from far off lands across the Cameroonian borders, maybe from Sudan. They came on horseback, heavily armed. They were expert horse riders and fully trained in the art of war. An Army battalion should be well trained to face these thieves. The United Nations should support Cameroon and the rest of Africa to protect these elephants and protected species. If these elephants are left only in the hands of Cameroon and Africa to protect, it might not go well. We lack the financial and technical means to do all what is necessary. The goal is to ensure environmental sustainability. The world is an ecosystem, and protecting the environment means protecting animals too. Water is the environment, and fish live in water. A forest is the environment, and elephants and other animals live in the forest.

The protection of water, animal and natural resources is a big challenge. Something has to be done to save them, in Cameroon, in Africa, in the entire world.

Look at the capital of China Beijing. You shall never see the clear sky there. Industrial pollution is everywhere. The sky is darkish bluish or darkish violet. The air is consistently dirty, and people suffer from lung diseases. Come back to Africa. Plastic bags lie everywhere and piles of trash The government of Cameroon has announced a band on nonbiodegradable plastics this from the year 2014. We hope all these measures work so that it will go a long way to protect the environment.

. In cities, water sources are used as dumping grounds. Much work is needed, from the Northern to the Southern hemisphere, about these problems, or else man is in danger. Things will not go well unless together we ensure environmental sustainability.

To sum it all up, it was really a great idea that the millennium development goals came about. He or she who brought the idea is a genius and I humble myself before them. No region, no country can live in isolation. Development must be balanced in all parts of the world so that the whole is in harmony. In other words, if the microcosm is in disharmony the macrocosm is equally in disharmony.

Take an example of somebody suffering from poverty and unemployment in Cameroon. Say he is fighting hard to go to America. Once there, he is partly the responsibility of the American government. Had he a decent job in Cameroon, he would not have gone to America. The number of illegal emigrants in Europe and America cannot be counted. They fear to return to their fatherlands because they fear misery and hardship. Some have even set themselves on fire right at the airport when just about to be repatriated. One sees the plane waiting for him. The time for his departure draws near. His heart beats. "Fatherland" equals "misery land." He dares not step on misery land, so he sets himself on fire.

This is a sign that rich continents and countries should also think of poor continents and countries. Whether we accept it or not, humanity is interconnected. And even within wealthy lands we have poverty and within poor places wealth. The suffering of a human being a kilometre or thousands of kilometres away will affect you in one way or another. We are all in this together.

The whole must develop coherently, or else there will be problems even where we hitherto thought it was good. Look at the 2008 depression and economic crisis that fell on Europe and America. This crisis caused many difficulties. The difficulties in Italy, Spain, Portugal, and Greece are enormous even until today. These countries will pick up eventually. But the fact that they have not yet made significant headway rings a bell. Who knew that Europe and America could be hit this hard? Africans should be reserved in thinking they have to migrate to Europe now. At first, when Africans went to Europe, they would sweep the streets and do odd jobs. However, today, young white men graduating from universities have to take over these jobs to support themselves. The black man does not have much to do in Europe now. I mean the blacks who want to migrate to Europe. If you were already in Europe before the crisis began, you might still be able to find your way, for home is home, "the universe is my home," home is everywhere. Many Portuguese are pouring into Angola, their former colony, to work there. The Portuguese government is encouraging the rich Angolan businesspersons to invest in Portugal.

Many Africans have the opinion that European and American grants do not help us. They say when Whitemen give us loans and aid, they know how to take it back again. Does it mean our leaders who negotiate these things are very foolish? If we so say, then we blame ourselves not others. Shall Africa remain the prodigal son forever? Angola is trying. She has gone a long way. If they hadn't experienced war under the warrior Jonas Savimbi, that country would be like New York or Paris today. Nonetheless, it is never late. They have come from behind and are doing so well.

Although Europe and America are facing crises, our problems have not disappeared. We have become accustomed to suffering, poverty, unemployment and disease. We were born in these conditions. We no longer complain. Those to whom we entrusted our country are in prison. The government has put them in prison until they pay the monies they embezzled from the state. So far, they have not paid back anything. Maybe we need to consult the oracle and see if they buried the monies, then we could dig it up. This is unfortunate. If they paid back this money, we would use it to develop our country. If the leaders who were supposed to build have specialized in breaking down the nation, how can we grow? So we have to stay on the same spot for a long time. We have dotted projects here and there. Small steps here and there. All is the elephant dance. You see our ministers and directors running up and down, working very hard and sweating, but very little changes after many years. We just turn around on the same spot. It takes a long time to build a nation. Everything is in limbo. We are in limbo.

Chapter 13
The Emergence of Carrefour Poli, the Emergence of Cameroon, the Emergence of Africa

An emerging economy or an emerging market is a nation with social or business activity growing rapidly and with industrialization. The economies of China, India and Brazil are the largest emerging economies, but there are other emerging economies like in Russia, Mexico, Indonesia, Turkey, South Africa, Argentina, Poland, Venezuela, and Malaysia. Depending on the criteria used to define emergence, the list can go up to fifty or sixty countries, but when you look at the list, hardly are African countries spotted. South Africa is unfailingly on the list. Sometimes we have Kenya, Senegal, Nigeria or Morocco, depending on the criteria used to measure emerging economies. This is a clear sign that Africa is a baby that has not yet learnt to walk. We shall walk one day, no matter how long it takes.

A report by the United States government says they do not expect a miracle – leading to dramatic change for the good– to happen in Africa in the next twenty years. But we must not take reports such as those as the conclusion of all things. They are judging us from existing conditions, which means if there are changes, we could see a lot of good. Take one example: if by some miracle all the ministers in prison decide to reveal where they hid state money, then by another miracle corruption and embezzlement is eradicated. With these two major achievements, Cameroon would, in a few years, be a paradise.

We are watching and studying the secret of how to emerge. When Africa shall pick up, we may grow at the level of China, with a double-digit growth rate each year. African leaders have predicted this. If our leaders are starting to predict when we will emerge, then they have seen such possibilities. We have the resources, and putting them to good use would make African economies emerge.

The top leaders of Cameroon have predicted the country will emerge by the year 2035. This year would be very interesting. Cameroon would not emerge in parts but as a block. It therefore means that the people of Carrefour Poli shall emerge along with the rest of the country. The following things shall be happening in Carrefour Poli and Cameroon as a whole.

By 2035, the growth in the gross domestic product (GDP) of Cameroon shall be very high. As is currently the case in China and some other emerging economies, Cameroon's growth rate is expected to rise to around 10% or more. Life will have changed in Carrefour Poli and Cameroon. Hopes will be very high.

By this time, Cameroon will be undergoing a tremendous change in industrialization, modernization and urbanization. There shall be very good things happening. During this time, Carrefour Poli shall be completely different from what we know today. With electricity, snakes will leave Carrefour Poli for the bush. There will be great improvements in both the quantity and quality of the water supply. Who knows, irrigated agriculture may become a practice all year round. Many young men and women of Carrefour Poli will travel to work in the industries that will have emerged like mushrooms all over the country. They will return home to Carrefour Poli with precious and beautiful things for their families and parents. The picture is amazing to look at. These good things will be happening all over Cameroon once the country as a whole has emerged.

The standard of living will improve. There will be a dramatic growth of the middle class. This newly born middle class will spend a lot of money on goods and services. This will help boost the industries to expand without limit. With the improvement in living standards, the people of Carrefour Poli will be eating better. Their food quality will improve a lot, and they will seek medical advice and easily pay their medical bills. And rather than mimic western development, we will come up with our own models of sustainable development that will inspire others.

By the year of emergence, Cameroon will have growing influence in world affairs. With strong economic power, Cameroon will have a powerful say in world affairs and in the world's organizations. Maybe a place at the Security Council of the United Nations? Moreover, who knows, it might be a daughter or son of Carrefour Poli representing Cameroon at the Security Council. Everything is so open and all possibilities are reachable.

As there shall be an increase in international trade, more job opportunities will be opened at home and abroad. Jobs will be available in all fields. Positions as engineers, nurses, doctors, teachers, translators, firefighters, pest controllers and more will be available. The businesspeople of non-English and French nationals will need Cameroonians who can speak Italian, German, Portuguese, Chinese and many other languages to translate for them.

However, we have to know that these things are attainable only when we set the goals and actively work to meet them. Those who have embezzled the nation's money, suffering now in prison, are bound to return these monies. This money, if paid, would be invested, and our targets might be reached. And if those in power now do not embezzle state fund, then it is a good sign for progress. All Cameroonians should work hard to see that this is attainable.

If Africa emerges as a block it will be good, because the problem of regional imbalance will be automatically resolved. We are all patient, humble and working very hard to emerge. We have a rendezvous to meet on the day of emergence. On this day in the year 2035, I shall go to Carrefour Poli as a witness of emergence. I shall go around, watch everything and compare to what we have now. If there are the expected changes, then Carrefour Poli has emerged. Carrefour Poli being the microcosm, it will mean the macrocosm (Cameroon) has emerged. How sweet! See you there!

Chapter 14
Conclusion

This is my experience of being a teacher in northern Cameroon. Other workers and teachers from the South have experienced life in other villages in the North. Different villages, different experiences. Some of my experiences may be similar to those of others, but some will be different.

I met some teachers who told me they have to walk across a river that comes up to neck level to reach their place of work. From there, going further, it is the border with Nigeria. There at the borders, none of Cameroon's mobile telephone networks reach. While there, you are cut off from the rest of your family in Cameroon. And too, the Cameroonian currency is not used there. Therefore, before arriving, you have to change CFA francs to the Nigerian naira. Moreover, the signals of the Cameroonian radio and television do not reach there. Therefore, you must learn to cope with Nigerian radio and television. I do not know if you can listen to BBC there.

It is government policy to prioritize development in the Northern region. Therefore, the government sends almost all newly recruited teachers to go and boost education in the Grand North as a whole. Until enough Northerners are trained as teachers to teach their own children, we from the South have to carry the burden of the Northern people's literacy and illiteracy.

Many teachers yearn for when it shall be possible for them to rightfully ask for transfers to go where they want. It is a matter of wait and see. Many things are expected to change as the country emerges. The railroad will be rebuilt, and new and faster trains bought, making it easier for teachers to travel to and from the North. Carrefour Poli and other northern villages will grow and develop. Sturdy and durable houses will be built in those villages. Electricity will be available. With these changes, workers will be able to work without many complaints. Salaries will be better than what we have now. We all work for the long awaited changes. We will grab them and hold them firmly. They must not slide off, for we have worked for them and they belong to us in this year of emergence – 2035.